CO060 62486

I0767611

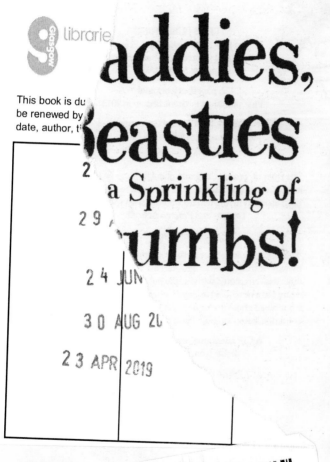

addies,
Beasties
a Sprinkling of
umbs!

For Mark, with love xx – TC
For E.M. Burton – AP

STRIPES PUBLISHING
An imprint of Little Tiger Press
1 The Coda Centre, 189 Munster Road,
London SW6 6AW

A paperback original
First published in Great Britain in 2013

ISBN: 978-1-84715-245-9

A CIP catalogue record for this book is
available from the British Library.

Printed and bound in the UK.

2 4 6 8 10 9 7 5 3 1

Baddies, Beasties

and a Sprinkling of

Crumbs!

Tracey Corderoy

Illustrated by Ali Pye

Inventions 384-389

Fig 384. Coggs

Clockwork cat
as pet for
Martha. Must
be lovable and
house-trained.

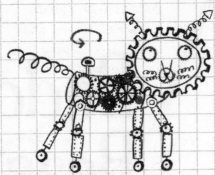

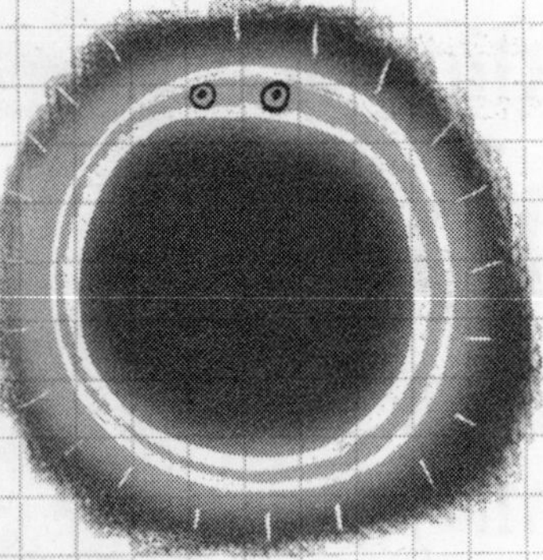

Fig 385. Rudolf

Bright blue fluorescent
circular frame for
making a hole appear
in a solid object. Hole
disappears when frame
is removed.

Fig 386. Tilly-Twirl

Blender to make
any flavour smoothie.
Just add milk then
programme in your order.

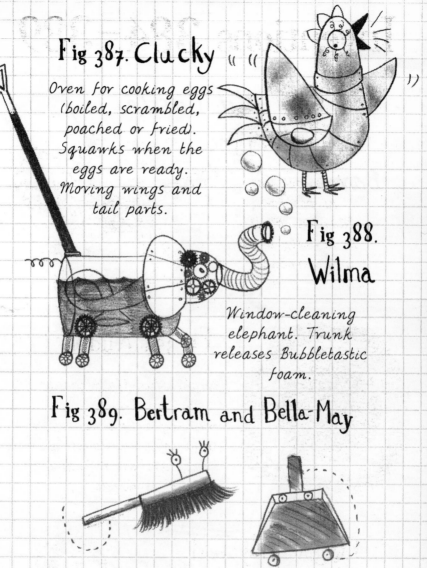

Fig 387. Clucky

Oven for cooking eggs (boiled, scrambled, poached or fried). Squawks when the eggs are ready. Moving wings and tail parts.

Fig 388. Wilma

Window-cleaning elephant. Trunk releases Bubbletastic foam.

Fig 389. Bertram and Bella-May

Dustpan and brush with automated wheels and bristles for super-speedy cleaning.

Property of Henrig Crumb

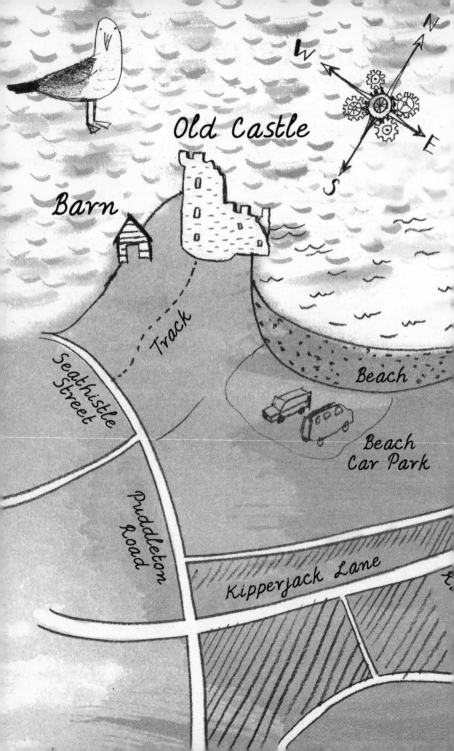

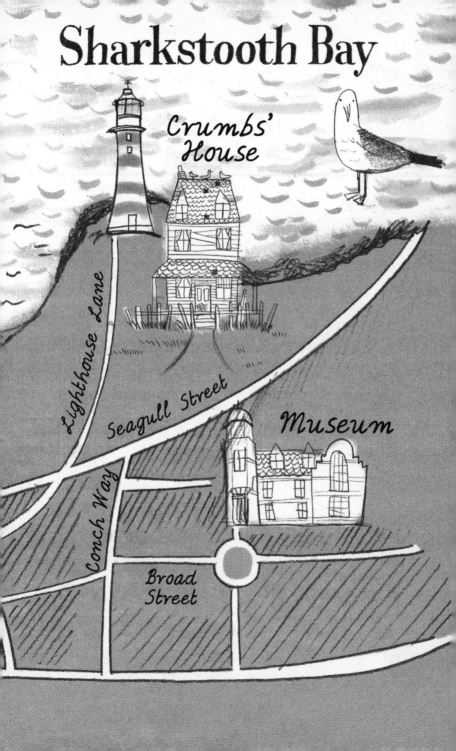

Martha, Otto and Scarlett Crumb were rather unusual children.

Martha was almost eleven, and the eldest Crumb. She had pale skin, chewed fingernails and mousy brown hair, which she wore in limp bunches. And she was a complete worrywart.

She worried about everything, from germs and fires to floods and plagues. She worried about forgetting to do her homework, even though she always remembered, and sometimes she even worried about *worrying*. But most of all, **Martha** worried about bad things happening to her family.

To make life sort of safe, Martha did wobbly handstands and cartwheels for luck, and made funny little creatures out of fluff.

She hoped that these lucky-fluffles would protect her family from bad things and bad people (even wicked goblins with pointy ears who could pop out of plugholes when you were least expecting them). She also wrote down happy words in her Happy Words Book to calm her nerves in particularly anxious moments.

Otto Crumb was nine. He was a skinny boy with white-blond hair, which had once been cut into a neat page-boy style, but had long since grown out. He had large pale blue eyes and very fair skin, like Martha.

Otto was a huge fan of TV detective Montague Plum. Even though Otto had seen every episode a hundred times or more, he never seemed to tire of watching them.

Just like Plum, Otto carried around a Solving Crimes Notebook, which he used to jot down the comings and goings of the street, or sketch anyone who looked, in his eyes, a little bit dodgy.

Scarlett, the youngest of the Crumbs, had just turned six and three-quarters. She had curly red hair that did as it pleased, a burst of freckles across her nose and, on her last count, three wobbly teeth.

Just like her hair, **Scarlett** did as she pleased. She was bold and fearless and a dab hand at karate. She ate peanut butter and jam sandwiches in the rain, growled through the letterbox at the postman, and she could pinch like a crab!

The children's mother, Clarice, had died last year, so now they just lived with their father, Henrig. Henrig was a world-famous inventor. In the past he'd invented many brilliant contraptions, as well as some gadgets for the home. His inventions were dotted all round the house, and those that they couldn't find a space for were stored down in the cellar.

The children had invented names for them all. There was **Wilma**, a window-cleaning robotic elephant that sneezed out jets of coloured foam, a blender, **Tilly-Twirl**, that made any smoothie you wanted, and a remote-controlled dustpan and brush called **Bertram and Bella-May**, who scuttled round sweeping up.

But best of all was Rudolf. Rudolf wasn't much to look at, but he was a very useful invention indeed. His name stood for **R**elative **U**ltrasonic **D**isplacement **O**f **L**ocation **F**rame. In other words, he was a magic hole!

Rudolf had a bright blue fluorescent frame, which allowed him to be folded up without getting lost. But when he was opened out, Rudolf formed a perfect circle, like a large frisbee. Then, when Rudolf was slapped on a wall, he made the bricks vanish, creating a magic hole to climb through.

Rudolf made holes in other things, too – fridge doors (for easy snacking), cupboards (for unloading mugs and plates), and wardrobes (for super-quick tidying up). He could make holes in pretty much anything.

Then there was **Coggs**, a clockwork cat that Henrig had made for Martha when she was a baby. In some ways, Coggs was just like any ordinary cat; he liked to be fussed over and tickled under his chin, and he spent a lot of time asleep. But he didn't *look* like an ordinary cat at all. Rather than having fur, he had cogs and springs. Coggs adored Martha, but strangers made him nervous.

The Crumbs lived in Lighthouse Lane, on the outskirts of Sharkstooth Bay. The other houses in their street were painted ice-cream colours, from shades of yellow to soft pastel pinks, and the gardens were all beautifully mowed and planted. Once upon a much happier time, the Crumbs' house had been painted a cool mint green.

But now the paint was peeling off and the garden was as overgrown as Otto's hair.

In the past, Henrig would have dealt with these things, but this year he hadn't been himself.

Henrig had always *looked* muddly. He'd always worn odd socks. And his shirts and waistcoats had never quite matched his trousers. But since Clarice died, Henrig Crumb had been muddly on the *inside*, too. He forgot little things, like what day it was, and bigger things, too (like Christmas).

For a time he'd even stopped inventing things. But as the months rolled on, the mountain of unpaid bills had forced him back to work.

And so today, as for the past ninety days, Henrig was locked away in his study working on something very important. He'd been commissioned by the curator of the town's museum to create an incredible *unbreakable* case. And in three days' time, a priceless ornament would be arriving at the museum to be displayed in Henrig's case. This ornament was a solid gold statue of an elephant, the size of a small cat, encrusted with precious jewels and worth *millions*.

Henrig had a few tests left to do on the case, and as he worked away in his attic room, the children made themselves breakfast. There was nothing terribly unusual about that, except that today was the first day of the summer holidays.

"So," said Otto, yawning widely, "do you think Dad will remember there's no school?"

Usually the children got themselves to school

after taking their dad a cup of coffee and the morning newspaper. But now six whole weeks lay ahead of them with nothing to do.

"Nah," said Scarlett. "He's probably forgotten. I'll bet you a half-chewed toffee he's forgotten to go shopping, too." She whisked a sticky half-chewed toffee out of her pocket.

The possibility of no food in the house sent Martha into a frenzy. "Forgotten to go shopping? *We'll starve!*" she cried.

Ignoring his sister, Otto took three eggs from a basket on the table and wandered over to Cluck 'n' Fry. "Who wants eggs then? We'd better eat while we can..."

"Me!" cried Scarlett.

"Yes, please," said Martha. "But make sure they're cooked. Undercooked eggs make you turn green. Then die."

Cluck 'n' Fry (or Clucky for short) was a mechanical chicken with an oven for a tummy and she made a mean fried egg. Otto popped the first egg into a hatch in Clucky's tummy and waited for the ear-splitting

SQUAWK!

that signalled Clucky had set about frying it.

A minute later, her wings started flapping.

"The first egg is ready!" Otto cried. "Get the plates!"

Quickly, Martha snatched up a plate, opened the hatch in Clucky's tummy and scooped out one perfectly cooked fried egg. She popped in the next one.

While the eggs were cooking, Scarlett made toast. She buttered it messily then slapped a slice on to each of their plates.

"After breakfast, we should go to the beach," said Scarlett, as they sat down to eat. "I'm going to dig a deep tunnel, right to Australia, and spend my holidays *there* catching crocodiles!"

"No!" wailed Martha. "Not the beach! What if you cut your foot on a shell and bleed to death!"

"That's nonsense," Scarlett scowled. "Otto, tell her we are going!"

But Otto had caught a glimpse of the front page of the newspaper. Dad's picture was on it. Why on earth would Dad be in the newspaper?

He picked up the paper and started to read as his sisters argued on...

"We ARE going to the beach!"

"No."

"Are, too!"

"Well, you'll be sorry if you die."

"You can't be *anything* if you're DEAD!" cried Scarlett.

Suddenly Otto put down the paper. His pale blue eyes were now big and wide and his heart was thumping fast.

"We can't go to the beach," he said. "Not today. Dad might be in terrible danger..."

Chapter Two

"What? Dad's in *danger*?" Martha cried. "From aliens? From plughole goblins? From WHAT?!"

Otto tapped the newspaper with his fork. "Look!" he said.

The story was about the Unstoppables, a notorious gang of robbers who travelled around the country pinching anything worth stacks of money from right under people's noses. It seemed that their next target was the Sharkstooth Bay Museum!

"Listen," said Otto. And he read out the article...

INVENTOR VS. UNSTOPPABLES

THIS SATURDAY, THE GOLDEN Elephant of Heera will be arriving in Sharkstooth Bay. It will be on display in the town's museum for the entire month of August.

Mr Doddery, the curator of the museum, is looking forward to its arrival, despite police worries that it will be a target for the Unstoppables. "I'm not bothered in the least!" laughed Mr Doddery. "As you know, the famous inventor Henrig Crumb is making a case to protect the elephant. A case not even those Unstoppables can break. Just let them try!

Henrig Crumb, Inventor

Martha and Scarlett looked blankly at Otto.

"Don't you *see*?" Otto cried. "It's been common knowledge for weeks that Dad's working on the case. But now it's like Doddery has set the Unstoppables a challenge to try and *steal* the elephant! And if they succeed, Dad won't get paid, and no money means ... no home."

"No *home*?" cried Martha, leaping up from her chair and attempting a wobbly handstand. "We'll be forced to live in a smelly field with mud and germs a-and *goats*!" She cartwheeled to the phone. "Quick! Call the police!"

"No," cried Otto. "No one's *done* anything yet! They can't solve a crime that hasn't been committed. Besides, our police are rubbish!"

Otto had a point. They couldn't rely on the Sharkstooth Bay police to protect any golden elephants. The only thing *they* were any good at was giving out parking tickets! They wouldn't know where to start with cunning robbers. And the Unstoppables were one serious gang of villains.

For as long as Otto could remember, the Unstoppables had been in the news. They'd burgled hundreds of stately homes and several dozen art galleries. Over the years they'd swiped treasures worth a fortune. And now the gang seemed to be targeting museums.

But no one knew what they *looked* like. Or how many of them there were. That was because they were masters of disguise...

Otto whipped out his Solving Crimes Notebook from his jeans' pocket and quickly scanned the pages. "Now I come to think of it, there've been some really odd people around lately. Remember those men selling double glazing?" he asked. "And those three ugly women who called last Friday, asking the way to the beach?"

His sisters nodded and Otto went on. "Well, *what if* those were the Unstoppables in disguise?"

Scarlett tutted. "Don't be stupid. You think *everyone's* in disguise. Last week you said you thought your teacher had been kidnapped and replaced by a *spy*. Just because he'd got a new pair of glasses!"

Otto ignored her.

"But, Otto," sniffed Martha, "I d-don't understand. Why would the Unstoppables want to come to *our* house?"

"To steal Dad's case, of course!" Otto cried. "Then, on Saturday, when that priceless elephant comes to the museum, there'll be no unbreakable case to protect it. So the robbers will be able to pinch it as easy as pie!"

Martha let out a horrified scream. "But that means they could come here *tonight*!"

"Exactly," said Otto, closing his notebook. "And that's why we can't just play on the beach.

We've *got* to be ready for them. We need to work out a plan, and fast."

As the children continued their breakfast they tried to think of some ideas. They hadn't got very far when Dad wandered in, still dressed in yesterday's clothes. His hair was unbrushed, he had dark circles under his eyes and a fine film of bristles covered his chin.

"Oh, Dad!" squeaked Martha. "You look terrible. Here, have the rest of my egg! We were going to bring up your news—"

"*Coffee!*" cried Otto, slipping the newspaper quickly under the table. "We were going to bring up your *coffee*."

Otto glared at Martha. The last thing Dad needed was to find out that a gang of cunning villains were after his case! This was something they'd have to sort out on their own.

Henrig hugged his children, then sat down at the table. "What would I do without you?" he said. "Now, I've been thinking about your summer holidays..."

"Oh! You remembered!" Scarlett piped up.

"Yes, indeed!" Henrig nodded. "But I was worried because I haven't got long to finish that case..."

The children exchanged nervous looks across the table.

"I didn't want you spending hours alone while I beavered away in the attic. And even when the case is delivered, I'll have to spend a lot of time at the museum. So anyway, I've invited your aunt to stay."

"What aunt?" Scarlett blurted out. "We haven't *got* an aunt!" And for once the children were all in agreement. None of them had heard mention of an *aunt* before.

"She's my sister, Bessie," Henrig replied. "She's been living in India, but now, well, she's back. We've exchanged the odd letter over the years. I told her when your mother ... you know. Then a few weeks ago she sent me a postcard saying she's back for good and living in the Highlands of Scotland. Apparently she's some sort of farmer

now. Anyway, she's coming."

"*When?*" cried Otto. A visiting aunt could get in the way of stopping the Unstoppables!

Henrig looked at his watch. "Um, anytime now. I've been meaning to tell you, but what with one thing and another..." His voice trailed off, as it did quite often these days.

"I-is she nice?" asked Martha hopefully. She missed their mum so much. Maybe this aunt would be a bit like her. Not *exactly* like her. No one could be that. But someone who might read them bedtime stories, mend the holes in their jumpers and jeans, and make macaroons and pancakes, maybe?

But before her father could answer, there came a loud knock at the door.

"Ah," said Henrig. "That must be her now."

Chapter THREE

The children followed their dad into the hallway. As he opened the door their jaws dropped and their hearts sank. There stood a dumpy old walrus stuffed into a thick tweed suit.

Scarlett wrinkled up her nose. "Ewww!"

Aunt Bessie was short, thickset and round. She was horribly hairy, too. Her suit was hairy. Her eyebrows were hairy. She even had tufts of hair sprouting out of her nostrils!

Around her tree-trunk-sized neck was a fat string of pearls, stretched so tightly they looked as if they might ping apart at any second. But worst of all, at Aunt Bessie's feet was an enormous travel bag. She was clearly planning on staying for some time...

Bessie peered up at her brother through narrow piggy eyes, her chins wobbling and her nostril hair twitching as she breathed.

"Henrig!"

she boomed like a cannon. **"How's my little brother?"**

Before Henrig could answer, Martha let out a shriek.

"G-goblin!" she gasped, pointing a shaky finger at a fearsome creature tucked under Aunt Bessie's arm. Martha spun round and was about to cartwheel off when Otto grabbed her hand.

"Martha," he whispered. "It's just a dog, don't worry."

Henrig quickly cleared his throat. "Hello, Bessie," he said. "Um, welcome!"

Bessie planted a kiss on her brother's cheek, nearly knocking him over. "How lovely to see you, Henrig!" she boomed. "After all these years!"

"Yes," said Henrig. "It has been quite some time."

He beckoned the children to come a little closer but none of them moved an inch.

"These are my children," Henrig said, his voice glowing with pride.

"And this is *my* baby!" thundered Aunt Bessie, holding up the ugly creature that had been tucked under her arm. "Meet Basil!"

"Oh," said Henrig, as the children eyed the beast. He was the ugliest dog they'd ever seen!

Just like his owner, Basil was hairy. He had short stumpy legs, a curly pig tail and two sharp, tusk-like teeth poking out of his jaw. And his eyes were beady and mean.

Suddenly he let out an ear-splitting squeal. The children all stuffed their fingers in their ears but Aunt Bessie simply patted Basil's head.

"There, there, Basie-Boo!" she cooed. She turned to her brother again. "Basil is a baby wild boar. Wild boars are very, um, *sensitive*. For one thing, they *really* don't like being gawped at!"

As if on cue, Basil let out a giant trump.

"See what I mean?" barked Aunt Bessie. "You're making him nervous!"

Henrig ushered his sister into the kitchen and the children trooped in behind. Their aunt hadn't looked at or spoken to them once.

"Cup of tea, Bessie?" Henrig asked.

"Nice and strong, with three heaped sugars!" boomed Bessie.

As Henrig popped the kettle on, Otto eyed his aunt. She looked bossy and interfering. The sort who would snoop. *Not* someone you'd want around when you needed to make top-secret plans to outwit a gang of criminals...

Aunt Bessie popped Basil on a chair at the table, then nosed round the kitchen until she found a clean saucer and a bottle of milk.

"Basil's thirsty, too!" she sniffed, pouring him out a deep saucerful. "There!" She beamed, putting it on the table before him.

As Basil started to gulp the milk, long strings of creamy dribble went flying through the air.

"Urgh!" cried Scarlett, as one landed on her nose. "*Gross!*"

Aunt Bessie wedged her huge bottom into the chair beside Basil and stroked him lovingly.

Henrig passed her a cup of tea. "So, Bessie, what have you been up to?"

"Well," she began, taking a deep slurp . "I was in India, as you know, searching out the tufty-tailed boar..."

Until recently, Bessie had been an explorer, seeking out ancient creatures thought to be extinct. Years ago, she'd embarked on a personal quest to find a tufty-tailed boar. For, despite what all the books said, she was certain that this creature still existed.

"I searched *everywhere!*" Bessie went on. "Up great hulking mountains, along windswept tracks, through deepest darkest jungles. But try as I might, I couldn't find one anywhere."

Scarlett yawned loudly but her aunt ignored her.

"Then about three months ago," Bessie continued, "I was at a market near the Hooghly River when I bumped into a couple from Scotland. They were touring India, you see. So, we got talking and they told me they'd seen tufty-tailed boars where *they* live! Right there in Scotland!"

"Really?" said Henrig.

"Yes! Can you *believe* it?" Aunt Bessie took another huge glug of tea. "They told me of a small cottage for sale on the banks of Loch Greythorn. *That's where the wee tufty-tailed boars live*, they said. So, I packed my trunk right away and took the first flight to Scotland. I bought the place the moment I got there and got myself a few wild boars!"

She told them that little Basil was her favourite. "None of their tails have turned tufty *quite* yet, because they're all babies, you see. But I'm *certain* Basil's tail will tuft at any second!"

The children glanced at Basil's string-like tail. No way would that bald piece of skin *ever* tuft!

Aunt Bessie chuntered on. "Soon I'm getting more baby boars. And I've got myself a farmhand, too, by the name of Donald McDonald. He's as skinny as a pencil and a bit of a drip, but he'll do!"

Aunt Bessie drained her teacup as the children watched from afar.

Suddenly they caught Henrig's eye.

"Bessie," he said, "*do* meet my children – Martha, Otto and Scarlett!"

Was it Otto's imagination, or did their aunt seem to *gulp* at the mention of them?

41

Aunt Bessie wiped her forehead, now dotted with cold beads of sweat. "I knew o-of Martha and Otto's births," she stuttered, "but had quite forgotten about Charlotte."

"I'm *Scarlett*! Not *Charlotte*!" Scarlett cried. "And I think aunts who forget people's names are silly!"

"Scarlett!" said Henrig, but the littlest Crumb didn't look bothered in the slightest.

"Scarlett! Be quiet or she'll *explode*!" Martha whispered. Her walrus-sized aunt certainly looked fit to blow up at any second.

Aunt Bessie gazed down at the three Crumb children, inspecting them one by one. Martha was fiddling with a ball of fluff. Otto was sketching her in his notebook. And Scarlett was wiggling a wobbly tooth.

Aunt Bessie had rarely met children on her lonely travels in India, and she *certainly* couldn't remember being a child herself, but she had come prepared.

She fetched her huge travel bag and heaved out a book. Quickly she flicked through the pages.

CHAPTER ELEVEN

CONVERSING WITH CHILDREN

A STEP-BY-STEP GUIDE TO BEING UNDERSTOOD

Bessie's eyes darted back and forth as she read to the bottom of the page. Then she snapped the book shut and cleared her throat noisily.

"He-llo!" she said in a slow voice, giving them all a wave. She seemed to think that children needed to be spoken to very loudly and very slowly, with hand gestures.

"I..." She prodded her hairy brown jacket. **"Am happy..."** She gave a huge smile. **"To meet you good little ... um ... children!"** She stabbed a sausage-like finger at them all.

As the children exchanged bemused looks, Aunt Bessie strode up and planted a hairy kiss on the top of each of their heads.

"Argghh!" Martha quivered.

"Hey," groaned Otto.

"Ewww!" cried Scarlett. "You're BEASTLY!"

Chapter FOUR

For the rest of the morning, the children watched Aunt Bessie (or Aunt *Beastly*, as Scarlett had named her) from a considerable distance. The last thing they wanted was another revolting kiss!

Henrig showed Bessie to her room – Otto's room – then disappeared back up to his study, promising to be down for lunch.

As Bessie unpacked, Basil chased Coggs, Martha's clockwork cat, all over the house. The beastly boar scurried around like a hairy little rocket, full of hot air and blasting wind.

"Come here, Coggs!" Martha cried, swiftly scooping him up. The children dashed into the girls' room and slammed the door.

"It's not fair!" grumbled Otto, as he set up an ancient camp bed in a tiny space beside Scarlett's bed. He dumped down some bits he'd quickly rescued from his room. "My bed will never stand *her* weight."

"Well, tell Aunt Beastly to hop it then!" Scarlett scowled.

Martha shrieked. "You can't do that! If she gets cross she'll *explode*! There'd be bits of Aunt Beastly all over the house!"

Scarlett wrinkled up her nose. That sounded gross. And so, for the next few hours, they kept out of their aunt's way and tried to figure out how to stop the Unstoppables instead.

Aunt Beastly was true to her word – she had come to help out, and "help out" is what she would do. At one o'clock she called them down for lunch.

As they trooped into the kitchen, a thick gloopy smell almost blew their socks off.

"Bleurghh!" said Scarlett. "What's the *pong*?"

"Please wash your hands," Aunt Beastly boomed in her slow, you-must-be-thick voice. She mimicked handwashing to help them understand. The children exchanged glances, but did as they were told.

Once Aunt Beastly had inspected their nails to check that they were spotlessly clean, she made them sit at the table, as straight as planks of wood.

There was no sign of their father.

He must have locked himself in his study, thought Otto. *And who could blame him?*

Aunt Beastly brought over some sandwiches on the best china plates. The children stared. They normally liked sandwiches. But these were cabbage ones! Sloppy green slime oozed out of the bread, making murky puddles on their plates.

"I will not eat a single mouthful," said

Scarlett. "So there!"

Aunt Beastly snorted and her wobbly cheeks inflated like two balloons. Martha gulped. Their aunt was about to blow up! She snatched up a soggy sandwich and begged Otto and Scarlett to do the same.

Rolling their eyes, they bit into the sandwiches. A sludgy river of ooze trickled on to their tongues. Otto and Martha had never tasted frogspawn before but Scarlett had (just the once) and this sandwich tasted just like it!

"You must chew it one hundred times!" barked their aunt, making a chewing action. **"That's what my trusty old book says!"**

With a satisfied nod, she thumped to the sink.

"Right!" said Scarlett, as soon as Aunt Beastly's back was turned. "No *way* am I eating this!"

She whisked Rudolf out of the table drawer, slapped him on the wall behind her, and slung everyone's sandwiches through the hole. They splashed into the garden pond with a sludgy *plop*!

"There!" whispered Scarlett, stuffing Rudolf away.

"Finished, Aunt Beast— I mean, *Bessie*!" Otto called to his aunt.

She bustled back over, looking delighted. Her old book was going to come in so useful! It had already given her this fine, healthy recipe, which the children clearly *adored*. There wasn't a single crumb on their plates! From now on, she decided, she would cook them cabbage for *every* meal!

While Aunt Beastly fed Basil some scrambled egg – "tail-tufting food!" – the children took care of the dishes.

Otto washed and Martha dried, standing as far from the sink as she could (because of her fear of plughole goblins). Then Scarlett put the plates away with a little help from Rudolf.

"Magic holes! Whatever next?" tutted Aunt Beastly, as she watched Scarlett lob the plates into the dresser.

After lunch the children retreated to their room to get to grips with their plan to stop the

Unstoppables. Otto took out his notebook and scribbled down the title:

Case 431: Scuppering a Robbery

"First," he said, "we need to jot down ways we can stop the Unstoppables getting to Dad's case in the attic."

"Easy!" said Scarlett. "I'll karate-chop them out of the house!"

The others didn't think much of this idea. The

robbers might be mean and muscly. Besides, Scarlett was only six and three-quarters.

"I think we need to be more cunning," said Otto. He thought for a moment, chewing his pencil like his hero, Montague Plum.

"Hmmm," he said. "In one Plum episode, this gang of robbers broke into a house, but they didn't know that the boy who lived there had got wind of their plan and had set *traps* to catch them!"

"What kind of traps?" Scarlett asked, twisting one of her wobbly teeth.

"For one thing," said Otto, "he'd left marbles on the floor. The robbers slipped all over the place. Then these nets came down and trapped them like wild animals."

"Cool!" cried Scarlett, but Martha was trembling. She leaped to her feet and threw herself into a series of wobbly handstands. All this mention of robbers and traps was *way* too worrying!

Ten handstands later, she flumped down on the bed, red-faced and panting.

Otto passed her her Happy Words Book. "Here," he said, "write some nice words. That always makes you feel better."

"Thanks, Otto," sniffed Martha, with a grateful nod. She began scribbling: Christmas, rainbow, pancakes...

Scarlett rubbed her hands together. "Okay, let's think of some cunning traps!" she grinned.

Suddenly her eyes lit up. "Why don't you make some fluffle-bats, Martha? We could dangle them down from the window frames. Then, if the robbers climb in in the dark, they'll feel those hairy things on their necks and run a mile!"

"Good idea," Otto nodded. But he doubted the robbers would run away *that* easily. The Unstoppables would be made of tougher stuff.

"We need something else, too," he said, "to confuse them and cause a commotion. Then we can bundle them down into the cellar and lock them away and call the police. Even *our* police should be able to cope with some trapped robbers."

"Good idea," said Scarlett. "I think we just need a few more booby traps."

"I've got some marbles," Otto said. "We could spread them all over the floor."

"And *m-maybe*," said Martha, quite shocked to have thought it, "we could put ... buckets of pond water ... on top of ... the doorframes? Um, then if the robbers pulled open a door..."

"*Kerrr-splat!*" sniggered Scarlett. "Then I'll karate-chop them down into the cellar. *Hi-yaa!*"

Now that the children had a plan, there was no time to lose. The Unstoppables might come

that very night.

Otto checked on Aunt Beastly. She was in the lounge, her head buried in her book. "The coast's clear!" he told his sisters. "Let's get started!"

"I'll stay in here with Coggs," said Martha. "It'll be my secret workshop!" She went to the wardrobe and pulled out an old pillowcase, full to the brim with fluff. "I reckon I'll need *all* this!" she said to Coggs.

The more Martha felt she had to protect her family, the bigger her fluffle creations became. These bats, she decided, would need to be giants!

Scarlett and Otto headed outside. Scarlett raced to the overgrown lawn to practise her karate moves while Otto found some buckets in the shed and filled them with dank green water from the pond. Then he carted them upstairs and hid them under the beds.

On his final trip, Martha showed him her bats. Each one was the size of a huge crow, with cardboard fangs and beady red buttons for eyes.

"They're great, Martha!" Otto said. "All we need to do now is go through our plan."

But where had *Scarlett* got to? She was supposed to be following with the last of the buckets. He wandered over to the window and glanced outside.

Scarlett was still in the garden but she wasn't alone. She was standing by the gate talking to three surfer dudes.

Otto had warned her countless times not to talk to strangers. And these three strangers looked decidedly stranger than most.

He hurried downstairs and out into the garden. "Scarlett!" he called. "You were meant to follow me in."

As he took the bucket of water from her, Otto glanced at the surfers. There was something not quite right about them.

Their clothes were okay – faded T-shirts, baggy shorts, flip-flops on their feet – yet *somehow* they didn't look like surfers. One was short and dumpy and looked more like a beach ball than a surfer! Another was lanky with a long, pointy nose and shoulder-length greasy hair.

The last of the three looked the oldest. He wore a shark's tooth necklace, which looked *way* too cool for him, and he had a mass of wavy blond hair – which didn't match his brown bottlebrush moustache at all!

Otto got the feeling he'd seen these men before, but he couldn't remember where. "Come on," he said to Scarlett. "Let's go in. Now."

"Okay, okay!" scowled Scarlett. "What's the hurry?"

Suddenly the dumpy surfer burped. "Um, pardon me," he said.

A moment later, Otto caught a whiff of cheese and onion crisps. And, as he did, he remembered something *very* important...

Last week, when those double-glazing men had called, one of *them* had stunk of crisps, too – cheese and onion flavour, just like this guy.

The older surfer stepped forward. "Hi there, um, little dude!" he said. "I was just asking your sis here if she had any glue we could borrow? One of our surfboards has just broken and it would be cool if I could just nip inside your house and

60

quickly just, um, fi—"

"No!" cried Otto. "We haven't got any!"

He grabbed Scarlett's arm and whisked her inside, locking the front door behind them.

"Let go!" she yelled, pinching like a cross little crab.

"Will you stop that?" Otto cried, bundling her upstairs to the bedroom.

"What's g-going on?" muttered Martha.

"*Don't ask me!*" yelled Scarlett. "Otto's gone *crazy!*"

Otto let Scarlett go and peeped through the window. The surfer dudes had vanished.

"*Otto,*" pleaded Martha, "what's the matter?"

Otto whipped out his notebook and showed his sisters sketches of all their recent "callers", pointing out the things they had in common.

"They were all the same shape and size, see?"

61

said Otto. "And one caller *always* has a bushy moustache – even that woman the other day!" At the time Otto had thought she was just unlucky, but what if she hadn't *been* a woman at all?

"And one *always* smells of cheese and onion crisps," muttered Otto, thinking very hard. "I think all these callers might have been the Unstoppables in disguise, trying to get into the house. We need to be ready for them tonight!"

Supper that night was cabbage soup. It smelled even worse than the sandwiches! Dad emerged from his study, and they sat round the table as Aunt Beastly ladled it into bowls.

"It looks like frog wee!" Scarlett groaned.

"*Scarlett,*" Henrig whispered. "Your aunt's trying her best, we must all be grateful."

He attempted to take their minds off the food with news of his invention.

"So, the case is almost finished!" he said. "Just a few last tests to do later." He swallowed a spoonful of lumpy soup and shuddered.

"Oh, jolly good!" Aunt Beastly smiled. "Glad to hear your work's going so well! So, how does the case actually *work*?"

"Um," said Henrig, gazing into his bowl. "It's ... complicated."

He attempted to tell her bits and bobs about the case, while the children battled through their soup. When their bowls were finally empty they trooped up to bed. The sooner their dad and aunt went up, the sooner they could put out the booby traps.

But Aunt Beastly, yet again, had other ideas...
She kept *insisting* she read them all a story. She
plonked herself on Martha's bed and opened a
very thick book.

"Your bedtime story tonight,"
she barked, **"is *The A to Z of Boars!*"**

A whole hour later she was *still* reading. The
children had heard all there was to know about
nasty little boars – from how to wash them and
feed them and walk them, to how to pick grime
from their trotters. They even knew how to
clean out their stinky ears!

"I actually *hate* boars!" Scarlett announced,
when, at last, her aunt closed the book.

"Shhh, Scarlett!" whispered Martha. "Or she'll
explode."

But their aunt did something *far* worse...

"Mwah!"

Scarlett felt a big hairy kiss planted firmly on her head!

"Mwah!"

"Mwah!"

Her brother and sister felt one, too.

"Goodnight!" boomed Aunt Beastly, bustling out and closing the door behind her.

"*Ewww!*" shuddered the children. "*Gross!*"

They waited until they heard Aunt Beastly close her bedroom door.

"Right," whispered Otto. "Torches on."

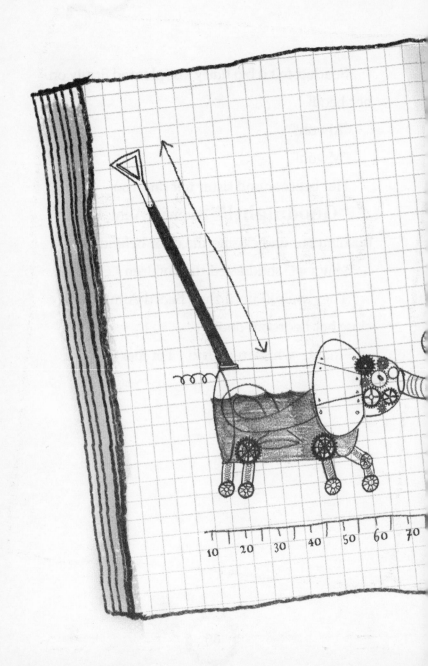

10   20   30   40   50   60   70

Sebastian Stinkerton was in a stinking mood as he picked at his greasy fish supper.

He hated grease.

He hated fish.

And he *really* hated the cramped red campervan in which he now sat. Of all the hideouts the Unstoppables had ever used, this nightmare on wheels took the biscuit!

They were parked near the end of Lighthouse Lane, keeping watch on the Crumbs' house. He'd been planning to steal Henrig's case for weeks but the story in the paper that morning had made him even more determined. If he could just get the case, stealing the elephant would be a doddle. That would show Doddery! How dare he challenge the Unstoppables!

Stinkerton shook his head. If *only* his partners in crime weren't such bumbling fools, that freckly girl might have let slip where her dad kept the case earlier.

"Why did you have to go and *burp*?" he snapped at Doug, who still wore his surfer disguise. "The *second* you burped, that blond boy freaked out – like he *remembered* the smell. Had you been stuffing crisps again?"

Dumpy Doug swallowed hard.

"As I suspected!" Stinkerton yelled.

"But, gov," said Doug. "Surely I'm not the *only* one who has something about me that them kids might remember." He nodded nervously at Stinkerton's face. "Maybe you should shave your moustache off."

"What?" roared Stinkerton. "Preposterous! I've had this ever since I was a baby!"

"You can't have!" cried Lenny. "Babies don't ha—"

"*What do you know?*" bellowed Stinkerton. "Anyway, *you* can't talk! Sort out that mop of greasy hair! I bet those kids have noticed *that!*"

Lenny frowned and Doug changed tack. "Sorry, gov, I didn't mean to scoff the crisps. I just ... forgot."

"*You forgot?*" snapped Stinkerton, banging the table and sending his fish flying. "Do you ever remember *anything*?"

"He never forgets where the fridge is!" laughed Lenny.

"Shut up!" yelled Doug. "May *I* remind *you* who lines us up all the best jobs? Who gets us all the good tip-offs, eh? Me!"

Stinkerton glared. Honestly! Doug was lucky to be an Unstoppable. It was only because he knew dodgy people who passed on useful information. Otherwise, all that Doug was good for was arguing with *Lenny*.

As for Lenny, he *did* have something that Stinkerton found *very* useful – a photographic memory. Lenny only needed to step inside a building to be able to tell you – weeks or months later – *exactly* where everything was. From the precise layout of an art gallery to the location of a vase in a mansion. If Lenny had glimpsed something *once*, he never forgot it.

Stinkerton glared at his two accomplices. They'd be nothing without *him*, the leader of the Unstoppables. According to Stinkerton (and he rarely got things wrong), he was the smartest crook alive.

Sebastian Stinkerton had been a robber ever since he was a baby. His dad, The Masked Whisper, had been a crook, too. He'd read to his toddler son every night from *The Robbers' Book of Robbing* and Stinkerton had lapped up every word.

By the age of five, Stinkerton was conning cash from the tooth fairy. When he was ten he could pick any lock in the land. By the time he reached eighteen, his house was crammed with priceless treasures.

Many years of happy robbing followed, but this elephant was to be Stinkerton's last job.

Then he'd flog a lifetime of stolen treasures, dump Lenny and Doug and live in the south of France in a mansion with diamond-studded gates and a whopping burglar alarm. But first he needed that golden elephant.

"Right," Stinkerton said with a nod. "We've *got* to get that case. Tonight."

"But, gov," moaned Lenny, "we still don't know where that inventor bloke *keeps* it, do we?"

Stinkerton fingered his moustache, thinking hard. Stealing that case *should* be easy for a robber as brilliant as him. And yet, there was something about those Crumbs that was making him feel very twitchy indeed.

The dad wasn't a problem. He was just muddly. But those *kids*. Now they spelled trouble.

And as if three pesky kids weren't enough, now a walrus of a woman had moved in, too!

And that little *monster* she'd brought with her. From what Stinkerton had seen of him shooting through the garden, his teeth looked as sharp as spears!

Stinkerton peered through the curtains. A light was still on in the Crumbs' attic room. Maybe *that* was where the famous inventor worked?

As Stinkerton watched, the light went off and the house was plunged into darkness.

"Right," he said. "Looks like they're all in bed. Time to get ready."

Chapter Six

The Unstoppables weren't the only ones to have spied the light go off in the attic. Otto was keeping watch at the foot of the stairs when the glow under the door suddenly went out. Dad was going to bed, at last!

Otto slipped behind the landing curtains as Dad wandered down the stairs and into his bedroom. Otto knew he'd be asleep in no time.

He tiptoed back to his sisters' room where the girls sat waiting, torches at the ready.

"Okay," Otto whispered. "Let's set the traps."

"About time!" Scarlett piped up.

"Shhh!"

They slid the buckets of pond water from underneath the beds and lugged them downstairs. Otto stood on a chair and reached up to balance them on the doors into the kitchen and sitting room. Martha, meanwhile, did *exactly*

76

twenty-five handstands and wrote three words in her Happy Words Book, before finally hanging up her giant fluffle-bats.

"Right, follow me," Otto whispered.

Clutching their torches, he led the way to the hall. Otto opened a drawer in a side table, took out three bags of marbles and the children quietly scattered them over the tiled floor. If the bats and the pond water didn't stop the robbers, these slippy marbles were *bound* to do the trick!

The children crept down to the cellar, where they planned to hide out. Then, if the Unstoppables *did* come, they would be ready for them.

Down the road a campervan door opened and the Unstoppables crept from their hideout. Stinkerton double-checked they had everything.

"Torches?"

"Check."

"Lock picker?"

"Check."

"Rope?"

"Check."

"Loot sack?"

"Check!"

"Anything we've missed?" Stinkerton asked.

"Maybe a midnight snack?" mumbled Doug.

"NO!"

They slunk down the lane, past all the neat houses until they reached the Crumbs' house.

"I spotted a kitchen window earlier," whispered Lenny. "Left side of the house, eight paces forward, turn right ninety degrees."

Stinkerton gave a nod. "Okay, follow me."

He leaped over the tatty picket fence, closely followed by Lenny. Doug, who couldn't leap for toffee, headed through the gate.

C-R-E-A-K!

"*What in the name of...* SHHH!" hissed Stinkerton.

They crept eight paces down the side of the house, turned and stopped at the kitchen window. Stinkerton rifled through the tools on his belt and took out his lock picker. Then, with a click and a snap and a clunk, he unpicked the window lock.

"Right, Doug first," whispered Stinkerton.

Dumpy Doug always needed a leg-up. Stinkerton and Lenny grabbed him by the collar, hoisted him up and stuffed his head through the window. Then they had to try and squeeze the *rest* of him through.

Bit by bit, Doug was jiggled through the window until he was almost in.

"Just one more shove should do it!" Stinkerton puffed.

But suddenly Doug felt something on his neck. Something big. Something hairy.

"Arggh!" he shrieked, as one of Martha's giant fluffle-bats tickled behind his ear. "There's something here! It's biting me! *Geroff!*"

"Stop shouting!" Stinkerton snarled.

"Yeah!" hissed Lenny. "*You'll wake up the whole house!*"

With that, Lenny booted Doug hard on the bottom and he popped through the window like a cork. Lenny dived in after him.

"*Nincompoop!*"

"*Lanky pants!*"

"*Great lump of stinky cheese!*"

"*Enough!*" snapped Stinkerton. "*Just be quiet!*"

He shot through the window and shone his torch at the frame. Three toy bats dangled down – fat and fluffy ... and harmless.

"Huh!" huffed Stinkerton "So! I was right – those pesky kids *were* expecting us. Well, it'll take more than *that* to stop the Unstoppables!"

Lenny and Doug scrambled to their feet and all three crept across the kitchen.

"Lenny," hissed Stinkerton, "memorize the layout."

They headed to the door leading into the

hallway. It was slightly ajar but, in the gloom, no one saw the bucket teetering on top.

Stinkerton's fingers closed round the doorknob. He was *just* about to edge it open when he heard footsteps on the stairs.

"Oh *dear*, Basie-Boo!" came a booming voice. "Do you need plopsies in the garden?"

"Blast!" muttered Stinkerton. The walrus-woman was coming!

He shone his torch round the room and spotted another door in the corner. "Quick!" whispered Stinkerton. "In there!"

As they tiptoed to the cellar door, an ear-splitting scream ripped down the hallway, stopping them in their tracks.

"Argggh!" Aunt Beastly screamed again, as the marbles on the floor sent her whizzing along like a rocket.

 83

Basil flew from her arms and hit the floor with a bump.

"No!" wailed Aunt Beastly, her arms waving wildly as she hurtled towards the kitchen door. **THUNK!** She hit the door, then slid to the floor and...

KERRR-SPLAT!

Stinkerton turned. In the torchlight, he could just make out the walrus-woman sitting on the floor with a bucket on her head. Cold slimy pond water seeped down over her shoulders, soaking her nightie in goo. This must have been yet another trap meant for *them*!

At that moment, Basil scuttled in from the hallway as more footsteps sounded on the stairs. It seemed like the entire house was now awake.

"*Time to leave!*" whispered Stinkerton.

They hurried to the kitchen window and stuffed Dumpy Doug through. Stinkerton then shot out after him. "Come on, Lenny!"

"But my cap's tangled up in a bat thing!" hissed Lenny, trying to yank it off.

"Leave it!" breathed Stinkerton. "Just get out!"

Lenny had barely dived through the window when Martha, Otto and Scarlett raced up into the kitchen from their hiding place in the cellar. It was dark but they could just make out an Unstoppable sprawled in the doorway with a bucket on his head.

"Hi-Yaaa!" yelled Scarlett, performing a karate-chop. "Take that, you smelly old baddie!"

Suddenly a shrieking Basil launched himself at Scarlett's pyjama leg. **"WHEEE! WHEEE! WHEEE!"**

"Get off! What's *he* doing here?"

Otto shook his head. "Never mind Basil! Look! We did it!" he cried.

"But where are the other two?" Martha asked, as the bucket-headed robber groaned.

"They must have got away," said Otto. "But at least we've got one! Let's get him down into the cellar. Quick!"

But suddenly a light was switched on in the hallway. Everybody froze.

A bleary-eyed Henrig picked his way through the marbles to the kitchen door. "What's going on?" he muttered, yawning widely. He rubbed his eyes. "Hold on..." he said, as the person sprawled at his feet managed to wriggle out from under the bucket.

Martha, Otto and Scarlett gasped. The Unstoppable wasn't an Unstoppable at all. It was *Aunt Beastly*!

"Oh, Bessie!" cried Henrig. "Wha— I mean, who? Martha, Otto, Scarlett, *explain yourselves*!"

Martha clamped a trembling hand to her mouth as Basil began racing round and round trumping.

"Will *someone*," said Henrig, "kindly explain why your aunt is … is … like *this*?" His sister didn't even seem able to *speak* any more!

"It wasn't my fault!" said Scarlett indignantly, her freckly nose in the air. "We thought she was an Un—"

"Stop!" Otto shot a hand to her mouth. "I mean," he said, "we were just playing – just acting out a scene from one of my programmes! Um, I-I was being Montague Plum a-and Scarlett, she was—"

"*P-playing?*" uttered their dripping aunt, who had found her tongue at last.

88

Everyone stared down at her.

"*Playing?*" she repeated again, blinking through tadpole slime. Tomorrow she'd consult her book and find some better games for them than *this*!

"Bed," said Henrig, "and we'll talk about this in the morning!"

As he fetched the mop and found his sister a towel, Scarlett and Martha sloped off to bed, tiptoeing through the marbles.

Otto was just about to go, too, when he spotted that the kitchen window was ajar. And a woolly black cap was hooked up in a fluffle-bat!

He edged across the room and pulled the window shut. Then he quickly unhooked the cap from the fluffle-bat and stuffed it in his pocket.

"Um, g-goodnight," Otto muttered, hurrying from the kitchen. "And sorry!"

He sprinted along the hallway, then took the stairs two by two. When he got to the top he pulled the cap from his pocket.

"So..." Otto whispered under his breath, "...the Unstoppables *were* here!"

His thoughts shot to Dad's case. Had they managed to steal it or had his aunt scared them away before they'd got the chance?

Otto raced to the attic room. The case was still there. But if the Unstoppables hadn't managed to get it *this* time, surely they'd be back. And they wouldn't be foiled by booby traps next time.

He'd have to think of something else, and fast!

Chapter SEVEN

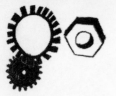

Otto was wide awake next morning when the sun peeped in at the window. He'd been working through an idea in his head, and suddenly...

"That's it!" he cried. He leaped out of bed and woke up his sisters. "Get up! I've had this great idea!"

The girls sat up and rubbed their eyes.

"So, what's the idea?" Scarlett yawned. "This had better be good."

"I'll tell you at breakfast," Otto said. "Come on!"

They got dressed quickly and tiptoed downstairs. Aunt Beastly and their dad were still asleep.

In the kitchen, Otto got started on breakfast. He popped three eggs into Clucky, then switched on Tilly-Twirl, who whisked them up some Sweetshop-Surprise-flavour smoothies.

As they sat round the table enjoying a meal containing no cabbage *whatsoever*, Otto went through his new plan...

"I'm going to phone the museum," he said. "I won't say who I am, but I'll tell them the Unstoppables are after Dad's case."

"But then they'll come and *take* it!" frowned Scarlett.

"Exactly!" grinned Otto. "I *want* them to take it. The only way to stop that case being stolen is to get it stored somewhere else – like the museum."

"B-but, Otto, are you *sure*?" Martha gasped. This was all so worrying! She whisked some fluff out of her pocket and began to make a lucky-fluffle hippo.

"Don't worry, Martha," said Otto. "I know what I'm doing."

Right after breakfast, Otto phoned the museum. He disguised his voice so Mr Doddery wouldn't think it was just a kid messing around.

"Hello," Otto growled. "You don't know me but I am a *man*. I thought you should know that the Unstoppables are planning to steal Henrig Crumb's case from his house. It would be safer in your museum. Er, goodbye."

Otto hung up. Wow, that felt good! He was thinking like Montague Plum. He always knew he was cut out to be a detective.

Ten minutes later, there was a knock at the door. Henrig, who had just appeared downstairs, went to open it.

"Mr Doddery!" said Henrig in surprise. Two burly museum guards stood at his side.

"Hello, Henrig," Mr Doddery whispered. He checked over his shoulder nervously before hurrying inside. The museum guards followed.

"Is everything all right?" asked Henrig, puzzled. Mr Doddery didn't seem himself at all – he looked edgy and pale and worried. "The case isn't due to be with you until tomorrow, is it?" Henrig said anxiously.

"Quite right," replied Mr Doddery. "But, for one reason or another, we've come to take it now."

"But—" said Henrig.

"No buts!" blustered Mr Doddery. "Just show us to it, will you? We have to get it back to the museum. It's for the best!"

Henrig showed them to the attic. The case stood on a platform in the middle of the room. It was about the size of a phone box with rows of

small cannons round its base. Built into the inside of the case was a smart white plinth for the golden elephant to sit on. There was a little sliding glass window for putting the elephant inside. As soon as it was in, the window would seal itself.

"Good!" muttered Mr Doddery. "It looks just right. Okay, Marcus, Greg – get it into the van."

The security guards picked up the case and carried it carefully downstairs, as the children watched silently from the kitchen doorway.

Henrig followed them outside as they loaded it into the van. He plied Mr Doddery with questions about why they were taking the case a day early, but Mr Doddery simply ignored them.

Back in the house, Otto made a call to the local radio station. Speaking in his growly man's voice again, he told them that he had it "on good authority" (Montague Plum said this a lot!) that the case had been moved from Henrig Crumb's house to a secure location until Saturday.

"Why did you do that?" Scarlett asked, when Otto put down the phone.

"Because," grinned Otto, "in five minutes' time it will be all over the breakfast news!"

"So?"

"So, the Unstoppables are *bound* to hear it and they'll stop trying to break in here! *And* they won't know where the case is, either."

Just then, Dad appeared, along with Aunt Beastly, who'd come down to make breakfast. She said she'd found a porridge recipe with cabbage and shrivelled prunes.

"We've already eaten," Otto beamed, "so you don't need to worry about us!"

As Henrig started to tell her about his case having been taken to the museum, he suddenly caught sight of the fluffle-bats.

"I think you owe your aunt an apology for last night," he said to the children.

"Sorry," they muttered, though Scarlett crossed her fingers.

Aunt Beastly nodded, then replied in her loud, slow voice...

"Don't worry, children. It is all forgotten."

"Bessie," said Henrig, "I must say, it's very good of you to forgive them so readily. I should also point out that *children*, you know ... er, do understand *normal* language."

"Humph!" huffed his sister. "That's not what my book says! My book also has something to say about 'play'." She opened it and read out the passage...

The act of play is, more often than not, misunderstood by small people. These small people (or children, as they are known) often indulge in frolicking frippery, naughty antics and misguided pranks. This they understand to be "play". Good, wholesome play, however, is quite another thing. It is necessary – if play is to be worthwhile – that it should be:

a) educational
b) of use
c) not in the slightest bit fun.

"I am taking the children on a hike," said Aunt Beastly. "Walking can be educational *and* useful and is, therefore, good play!"

"How does she work *that* out?" muttered Scarlett.

"Sssh!" whispered Martha. "Or she'll explode."

"I-I don't think I can join you," said Henrig quickly. "I need to go to the museum and carry out my final checks."

"Of course!" Aunt Beastly smiled, her nostril hair twitching. "We shall manage on our own, don't you worry! We shall walk the whole length of the beach – from one end right to the other. Dear little Basil will love the fresh air!"

"*What?*" groaned the children.

"Wellies on!" boomed Aunt Beastly, peering out of the window. "It looks like it's about to pour with rain!"

Chapter EIGHT

As the children and their aunt began their hike, the heavens opened. A great river of rain tumbled down as though the sky had a dreadfully runny nose. Otto, Martha and Scarlett were soaked to the skin before they'd even reached the beach, but there was no way their aunt was turning back.

A little way down Lighthouse Lane, the Unstoppables were having breakfast in their campervan.

"Any more sausages, gov?" asked Doug, gulping down his last mouthful.

"No!" snapped Stinkerton. "Now shush! I'm listening to the radio!" Stinkerton liked to keep up with local news when he was doing a job. It helped him know exactly what was what.

He turned up the radio to drown out the rain, just as the news began...

BREAKING NEWS!

We've just heard an interesting
development concerning Henrig
Crumb and his unbreakable case.
We have recently been tipped off –
and can now confirm – that the
case has been *moved* to a secret,
secure location ahead of the arrival
of the Golden Elephant of Heera
the day after tomorrow.

"*What?*" roared Stinkerton, banging the table.
"It's been *moved* – from right under our noses.
I bet those *kids* had something to do with this!"

He shot to the window but the rain blocked
his view. "I can't even *see* the Crumbs' rotten
house through this!"

"What shall we do, gov?" asked Lenny.

"I can sort it out!" cried Doug. "I can ask one
of me dodgy mates if they know where it's gone.

Henry Gibbings owes me a favour. I'll ask him."

"Shut up!" hissed Stinkerton. He couldn't think straight with those idiots jabbering on. He paced back and forth as the rain pelted down. Finally, he came to a halt.

"Right!" he barked. "This is what we'll do. Doug, you pay Henry Gibbings a visit, while Lenny and I go and suss out the museum. If we can't find the case before Saturday, we might have to try and swipe the elephant when it's *inside* the case."

"But that's impossible!" Lenny said.

"The case is unbreakable," added Doug.

"I know that, you idiots!" Stinkerton snapped. "But we might have no choice! Now, enough time-wasting! Lenny – *just drive!*"

Lenny jumped into the driver's seat, started up the engine and put his foot down hard.

KERR-JUDDER, KERR-JUDDER, KERR-JUUUNK! went the van, lurching to a stop.

"What's wrong?" yelled Stinkerton. "Are we out of petrol?"

"Nope," shrugged Lenny. "I just filled it up with a tank of nicked petrol!" He turned the key again but this time the van wouldn't even start.

"Well, what are you waiting for?" Stinkerton yelled. "Go and check the engine!"

They hurried out into the pouring rain to took a look. The van was clearly leaking – the engine was swimming in rainwater.

"The spark plugs are soaking!" Stinkerton cried. He rounded on Doug. "This is your fault! Of all the vans you *could* have swiped, you had to choose *this* heap of junk!"

"Well, I thought it was okay," shrugged Doug.

Stinkerton completely ignored Doug. "Now we're stuck here until it stops raining and those infernal spark plugs dry out!"

He spun round and squelched back into the van, slamming the door behind him.

"Temper temper," muttered Doug.

"Come on," said Lenny. "Let's get back inside."

Meanwhile, on the beach, a soggy group trooped on through the raging storm. Aunt Beastly marched forward with Basil tucked under her arm. Martha, Otto and Scarlett trudged along behind her with their heads down.

As their wellies overflowed with water, Aunt Beastly ushered them into a cave.

"Let's look for stalactites!" she said in her loud, slow voice.

"I've had enough of this!" yelled Scarlett, rain dripping off her freckly nose. "We *can* understand normal language!"

She recited the whole of *The Owl and the Pussycat* so that her aunt got the message.

"Oh!" said Aunt Beastly, looking quite shocked. "Um ... well, yes ... so I see. That was a very long poem, and I must say, very well said!"

"So speak to us *normally* then!" cried Otto.

"And we'd much rather get home," scowled Scarlett, "than hang around in this stinky cave!"

"Don't make her cross... Don't make her cross," chanted Martha.

For a moment, Aunt Beastly looked taken aback. Then she tucked Basil under her raincoat and pulled down her hat. "Well, if that's what you'd prefer, we'd better get a move on!"

And she strode out into the pouring rain...

As soon as they got home, they dried themselves off and Aunt Beastly served up another disgusting lunch.

Martha still felt shivery and went to bed immediately to, *hopefully*, ward off pneumonia. "See you all later," she sniffled. "*If* I'm still alive."

Otto and Scarlett did not feel close to death, so they each went off to do other things. Scarlett hung out in her top-secret den – upstairs in the airing cupboard where she'd squirrelled away her secret stash of toffees and chocolate.

Otto headed straight to the lounge, his Solving Crimes Notebook at the ready. He needed to watch an episode of *Montague Plum's Mysteries* to get more sleuthing ideas. If the Unstoppables came back, he needed to be ready!

Meanwhile, polish and duster in hand, Aunt Beastly went into a cleaning frenzy. She programmed Bertram and Bella-May to sweep the house from top to bottom, while she herself cleaned out the cupboards and drawers.

Otto managed to watch three whole episodes before heading to the kitchen for a drink. He opened the door, then stopped in his tracks. "Whoa!"

Aunt Beastly had slapped Rudolf on to the wall and was lobbing things through the hole he'd made into the front garden.

"Stop!" cried Otto, as old toys and teddies crash-landed on the lawn.

"Clutter!" sniffed Aunt Beastly, delving into the dresser and flinging out an old bear of Scarlett's. "Mess and muddle! In every cupboard. In every drawer! I *just* need to get it out of the house, then I'll scrub down the dresser before supper. Could you go and bag it up? Then we can take it to the tip."

"*No!*" shouted Otto. "Those are our *things!*"

He saw a painting he'd once done for his mum floating in a puddle. All the colours were running into each other in fuzzy blotches.

Otto felt his eyes sting. He blinked, then raced to get his sisters. No *way* were their memories being bagged up and chucked away.

Otto wasn't the *only* one surprised by the hole in the wall. Sebastian Stinkerton had now mended his van and was *just* about to drive out of Lighthouse Lane when he stopped.

"Lenny! Doug! Look!" he hissed, pointing out the hole.

"So?" muttered Doug. "It's just a hole."

"He's right," Lenny nodded. "For once!"

"Don't just look at the *hole*," cried Stinkerton. "Look at what's *made* it, idiots."

"But that's just a shiny frame," shrugged Lenny.

"I think you'll find it's much more than that!" Stinkerton smiled. "I mean, *look* – that shiny frame has made a hole in the wall. And if it can make a hole in a wall, it can make a hole in *anything*..."

A new plan was forming in his head. "We need to get our hands on that hole," said Stinkerton. "Then we'll go to the museum on

Saturday night, pop the hole on to the case, and whisk the elephant through it, easy as pie."

"Let's pinch the hole tonight!" cried Doug.

"Not so fast!" said Stinkerton. "We messed up big time last night – we can't afford any more mistakes!" He twirled his moustache thoughtfully. "Let's just lie low today, so that the kids think we've given up. Then, when the dust has settled, we'll get that hole!"

They watched as Martha, Otto and Scarlett gathered up the old toys from the grass. Then they saw them climb back through the hole, dragging the frame in behind them. The hole in the wall disappeared at once.

"Look at that!" Stinkerton nodded. "Totally brilliant!"

That night Dad came home just as supper was served – a foul-smelling cabbage casserole.

As the children picked through the soggy mess, Aunt Beastly plied Dad with yet more questions about his case.

Henrig told her this and that, in between stifled yawns. "It's been all go at the museum," he said. "Mr Doddery is panicking, as lots of staff have come down with some sort of flu bug, and with the elephant arriving in two days' time he'll need all the staff he can get! He's putting an ad in the paper, apparently."

Henrig stretched. "Anyway, enough about me! What have you been up to, Bessie?"

But his sister seemed suddenly deep in thought.

"Bessie?"

"Oh!" Aunt Beastly jumped. "Me? Up to? Let's

see... Well, I've made a start on the cleaning..."

"Ah, yes," said Henrig, gazing around at the spotlessly clean kitchen. "I thought something looked different. Thank you."

Normally the drawers had piles of bills poking out, but now there was nothing in sight.

Their aunt had no right to snoop around their stuff, thought Otto.

Henrig forced down a little more casserole. "So, anyway, I'm back at the museum tomorrow. Can you stay with the children?"

"But I ... need to go, um ... somewhere ... in the morning!" Aunt Beastly said very jerkily.

"Oh," Henrig nodded. "No problem at all! I'll look after the children until you're back then."

It didn't go unnoticed by Otto that since his dad had mentioned the museum, Aunt Beastly had looked on edge. Now she was fiddling with her necklace and her cheeks had turned beetroot. It was almost as if she had something to hide...

Otto was still puzzling about this as he lay in bed later. If his aunt *did* have something to hide, then he would discover it.

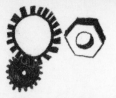

O tto woke up on Friday morning with butterflies in his tummy. Tomorrow the Golden Elephant of Heera was arriving at the museum.

Dad would be spending most of the day there, getting everything ready. And Otto felt sure the Unstoppables would be watching.

Then there was Aunt Beastly. Where was she off to this morning? She hadn't given them any clues last night. This was definitely something that needed investigating.

A floorboard on the landing creaked. Otto jumped out of bed, hurried to the door and peeped out. Aunt Beastly was tiptoeing towards the stairs with Basil under her arm. *That's odd,* thought Otto. *Normally she thunders everywhere.*

He waited until she'd gone downstairs, then crept to the top of the landing. He could hear her talking in the kitchen so he padded down and listened at the door.

Aunt Beastly was on the telephone. Her voice was low and quiet. "Yes," she said. "Hmmm, that's right. Well, I could come and meet you this morning. I'm sure I could be just what you need. I know *so very much* that you'd find useful..."

"I know so very much..." Otto said to himself. What was it that she knew so much about?

Suddenly it came to him. At supper last night Aunt Beastly had gone out of her way to learn all about the unbreakable case. But who could she want to pass *that* information on to?

"*The Unstoppables!*" gasped Otto. It had to be.

"And what about the *money*?" Aunt Beastly said. "No. I'd need more than that! What? Er, well, that sounds a *bit* more like it. I'll see you at ten. Goodbye."

Otto scurried silently back upstairs and shook his sisters awake. "Martha! Scarlett! Listen!" he panted. "Aunt Beastly's going to meet *the Unstoppables*."

"What?" squeaked Martha.

"No, she *isn't*," Scarlett groaned. "You're just imagining stuff again!"

"*I'm not!*" cried Otto. "I'm telling you, she's in cahoots with the Unstoppables! She wants us to believe she's here to help us, when really she's decided she'd be far better off helping *them* steal that elephant instead! I just heard her on the phone – she was asking for money in return for information. Information about Dad. Information about the case. Information about everything!"

"So, how would she get the baddies' number?" yawned Scarlett.

122

"What?" said Otto. "I ... I dunno! She just ... *did*. She's a lot sneakier than you think."

"But she's our *aunt*," Martha wailed. "Aunts aren't meant to be robbers! They're meant to make pancakes a-and knit blankets."

"Well, *our* aunt is a *robber*," said Otto. "So there!" He snatched up his clothes off a pile on the floor. "Hurry up and get dressed!" he said. "We need to follow her to the Unstoppables and find out exactly what they're up to."

Otto rummaged around in his rucksack. "I need to find Ear and Wig," he said. "I'm pretty sure they're in here somewhere."

Ear and Wig were electronic bugs Dad had invented for Otto's seventh birthday. They looked like earwigs but were really tracking devices.

The underside of Ear's body had lots of

special hooks on it so that he could be stuck on to anything. And once Wig's pointy tail bits were plugged into a small tracking screen, it would show a detailed map of *exactly* where Ear was.

As long as Ear and Wig were within twenty miles of each other, you could track a person's every move!

Otto dug deeper into his rucksack and finally found them. "Okay," he said, looking at his sisters. "Now we've got to get Ear on to Aunt Beastly. Then we'll be able to track her."

"B-but how do we do that?" Martha gulped, already fearing the answer. To get Ear on to people meant you had to get *close* to them.

Otto thought. There was really nothing else for it. "One of us will have to ... hug her," he said.

"*Hug* her?" gasped Martha.

"No way!" Scarlett scowled.

"*How else can we do it?*" cried Otto.

Scarlett folded her arms and Martha turned white.

"Okay, okay, I'll do it!" grumbled Otto. "But just make sure she doesn't squeeze me to death."

"To death?" shrieked Martha.

"No, just— Oh, never mind!"

They trooped downstairs, Ear at the ready in Otto's clammy hand. The thought of hugging his aunt turned his stomach even more than cabbage!

Aunt Beastly was in the hallway, heading to the front door.

"Wait!" shrieked Martha.

"Yes?" said Aunt Beastly, turning round. Her nostril hairs wiggled like two fat caterpillars.

"Do it, Otto – *quick*!" Scarlett whispered. She gave his ankle a little kick.

Otto shuffled on the spot, then tried to speak, but a jumble of gurgles dribbled out instead. "Eee ... aaahh ... gooo..."

"He wants to give you a hug!" cried Scarlett. "Because ... because ... he loves you!"

"A-and he'll miss you when you go out!" Martha blurted bravely.

Aunt Beastly stood rooted to the spot.

"You'll miss me?" she said finally, her eyes now on Otto. She slowly tipped her head from side to side, as if she didn't quite understand.

"Er," said Otto, in a quavering voice. "Um, kind of."

126

If he was *going* to do it, he thought, then best to just go for it quickly. He held his breath, then belted towards his aunt, his arms outstretched!

Aunt Beastly was nearly knocked off her feet as Otto's head butted her big, round tummy.

"Oh, well ... I'll be back soon!" she spluttered. "Um, there, there! Don't be sad!"

She patted his head and Otto sprang back. *He'd done it!* Ear was now stuck to the back of her jacket.

Suddenly Aunt Beastly leaped towards them, her lips puckered up for a kiss.

"Ewww!" shrieked the children as they dashed upstairs.

"Oh!" Aunt Beastly frowned. "Well, bye bye, then! Look after Basil while I'm gone!"

"We will!" the children called down.

As soon as they heard the front door close, Otto pulled Wig out of his pocket and plugged his tail bits into the tracking screen.

Bleep! The screen lit up at once and a map of Sharkstooth Bay appeared. As they stared at the screen, a flashing red dot appeared on Lighthouse Lane.

Lighthouse Lane

Seagull Street

Museum

Conch Way

Broad Street

"That's her!" cried Scarlett. "Let's follow!"

"Not yet," said Otto. "She's still too close." Montague Plum always waited a bit before he tailed his suspects. "Let's grab some breakfast first."

They hurried downstairs and into the kitchen. "No walkies for you today!" said Scarlett, dumping Basil out in the garden.

Otto popped an egg into Clucky's tummy while Martha got some plates.

"Where's Aunt Beastly now?" she asked, resisting the urge to do a quick handstand.

Otto checked the screen. "She's heading along Seagull Street."

As they wolfed down their breakfast, they kept their eye on Wig's screen. The red dot was moving quickly now. From Seagull Street, it turned right into Conch Way.

"Okay," Otto nodded. "*Time to go!*"

T he children raced to the door.

"Wait!" cried Martha. She scribbled a note to Dad, who was already hard at work in the attic, and left it on the kitchen table.

"Right," said Otto impatiently. "Follow me!"

They hurried outside and along the lane, passing the red campervan where Stinkerton was keeping watch.

"Hmmm," he murmured, twirling his moustache, "the walrus-woman has already gone out and now the kids are off, too."

"Time to steal that hole?" asked Doug.

"No. The inventor's at home. And anyway, we need to go and get to grips with the layout of the museum. If we're stealing the elephant tomorrow night there's still lots of planning to do. They're bound to go to the museum in the morning when the elephant arrives – we'll swipe the hole then."

The children sped along the streets, tracking their aunt all the way into town. She visited the supermarket, then the pet shop next door.

"I thought you said she was meeting the *Unstoppables*," Scarlett said with a frown.

Otto shrugged uncertainly. "Well, she's probably just doing some shopping on the way."

Finally, the flashing red dot headed down Broad Street and towards the museum.

"Look!" cried Otto. "She must be meeting them there!"

As they hurried along to Broad Street, Martha was getting twitchy. What if the Unstoppables caught them spying? What if they locked them in some damp, dark dungeon forever!

To protect her family, she started dodging

the pavement cracks. After all, it was an absolute fact that stepping on cracks brought dreadful bad luck. The problem was, there were cracks in the pavement *everywhere*.

"Get a move on, Martha!" Otto cried, as a bright red campervan sped by. As he glanced at it, Otto thought it looked identical to the one they'd passed on Lighthouse Lane. He would have to check his notebook later.

"Eeek!" squeaked Martha, skirting round a huge crack, then hopping over three more.

"Martha, what are you *doing*?" scowled Scarlett.

"Don't step on the cracks!" yelled Martha.

By the time they *finally* reached the museum, their aunt was already leaving. The children nipped behind a bush as she marched past.

"We've missed the *meeting*!" groaned Otto.

As he spoke, he spotted the red campervan parked nearby. "And there's that van again!" Otto scribbled it down in his notebook.

"I'm really sorry," Martha sniffed. "It's my fault we missed the meeting."

"You and your silly cracks!" snapped Scarlett. "But wait – we could *still* sneak into the museum and spy on the Unstoppables."

"We can't," sighed Otto. "If Aunt Beastly's going home, we need to get there before *she* does. Otherwise she'll suss that something's up. Come on, let's go."

The Unstoppables' trip to the museum had gone very well. As they returned to their campervan, Stinkerton was positively glowing. "So, Lenny – you've memorized the *entire* layout of the

135

museum? You know *exactly* where *everything* is?"

"Sure do, gov!" Lenny nodded. He'd memorized every single inch of the museum. He even knew the distance in paces from the café to the loos!

Stinkerton took out a smart silver scrapbook and began to write something inside. He liked to keep a record of all his jobs so that, when he was old and grey, he could share the lovely stories with his grandchildren...

Those Crumb kids will never outwit me. Tomorrow's the day I scoop the biggest prize of my sparklingly brilliant career.

When Otto, Martha and Scarlett got home, Dad was still up in the attic working. Martha threw her note away, then they scooped up Basil's poop from the garden and let him back inside.

"We must pretend we've walked him, too," said Scarlett, "or Aunt Beastly will make us do it later."

"Yeah," groaned Otto. He was reading through the clues he had noted down so far.

"So, um, about the Unstoppables..." said Martha. "You're sure that Aunt Beastly's one, too?"

"No question about it!" Otto said quickly. "And that means it's more important than ever that she finds out *nothing* else about Dad's case, as she'll tell her gang everything."

His sisters nodded.

"And," added Otto, "we have to act normally. Like we don't know a thing. So, even though we know she's a rotten double-crosser, we have to pretend like nothing's happened, or she'll be on to us, right?"

Martha and Scarlett nodded again. It would be hard but they'd try.

Ten minutes later, their aunt appeared. She swept into the kitchen looking smug. A weird noise was coming out of her mouth. "Leee-aaa-aaa-aaa-aaa-aaa!"

"Are you all right?" Martha asked her aunt. It sounded like she was in pain. But it turned out that Aunt Beastly was simply singing.

"We've got to get Ear off her back," whispered Otto.

"I'll do it," said Scarlett quickly.

138

Grinning widely, she sprang into action. She crossed the room in a series of mad karate moves and kicked Ear off her aunt's back.

Aunt Beastly suddenly stopped singing and peered at Scarlett suspiciously.

"Um, Scarlett's missed you, too!" said Otto.

"Oooh, she *has*!" gulped Martha. "She always does karate when she m-misses people."

Aunt Beastly tilted her head to one side. "Goodness!" she said. Now *two* people were missing her. "So, what have you been up to while I've been gone?" she asked.

"*Walking Basil!*" the children said at once, their fingers crossed tightly behind their backs.

"Really?" Aunt Beastly replied. She glanced down at Basil, who was chasing his tail. "He doesn't *look* very tired! I think, after lunch, he might need a *longer* walkies. But don't worry, I'll come, too! I don't want you missing me again!"

Supper that evening was a huge cabbage pie, followed by a vile cabbage jelly. Aunt Beastly looked very pleased with herself as she took her place at the table. Otto was desperate to know what she and the Unstoppables had been plotting at the museum.

They struggled through the pie but then had to tackle the murky green jelly. Dad, as usual, tried to take their minds off the food.

"So, anyway – my case is in position," he said, "but the sprinklers on the ceiling kee—"

"DAD!" Otto quickly cut in. "Isn't this jelly so yummy?" He had to change the subject before his dad gave anything away. "I love, love, LOVE cabbage jelly!" he yelled.

"M-me, too," muttered Martha, shuddering.

"Yeah, okay... And *me*," scowled Scarlett. "But no seconds, thanks!"

By the time everyone had finished their pudding, the smirk that Aunt Beastly had worn through the meal erupted into a great hairy smile.

"Oooh!" she exclaimed, *all* her chins wobbling. "I have a wonderful surprise to end the meal!"

"We're full!" the children quickly cried.

"No, no!" giggled Aunt Beastly. "It's not more

food. It's – well – I've got myself a job!"

"Oh!" said Henrig, surprised.

"What's she up to *now*?" Otto whispered to his sisters.

"It's at the museum!" Aunt Beastly went on. "Henrig – do you remember last night when you said that they needed more staff?"

"Um, yes," Henrig nodded.

"Well, that got me thinking. I know *such* a lot about India, and I've read all about the Golden Elephant of Heera. So, anyway, this morning I went to see Mr Doddery and ... he gave me a job!"

Henrig opened his mouth, but before he could speak, Aunt Beastly barked, "Don't worry, though, dear – it's not full-time, so I'm sure between us we'll be able to look after the children! I just thought the extra money would come in handy... You do seem to have quite a pile of unpaid bills. And it means I'll be staying for the *entire* month of August!"

"I *told* you she wasn't an Unstoppable!" snapped Scarlett, as they trooped upstairs to bed. But

Otto still wasn't convinced.

"Don't you see? She's trying to trick us!" he said. "Yes, she went to the museum to get a job – but I *bet* she met the Unstoppables there, too! Just think how useful she'd be to them if she was *working* there."

"But—" said Scarlett.

"No buts!" cried Otto. "She wants us to *think* she's staying to help us, but she *isn't*, you'll see! The Unstoppables are going to try and steal that elephant and Aunt Beastly is in on it, too. Then *they'll* sell the elephant and disappear until *she* joins them at the end of August to split the cash. That way she won't blow her cover! See?"

Otto had to give it to her, their aunt was cleverer than she looked.

"So w-what are we going to do now?" sniffed Martha.

"Watch her!" cried Otto. "She'll lead us to her gang and then when we catch them red-handed there'll be no more Unstoppables – all *four* of them will be carted off to jail. But *until* then, make sure you don't say a thing to Dad – he's got enough on his mind already."

Otto thought of Montague Plum – some of his cases were mighty tricky but he *always* got the baddies in the end. "We're going to catch these crooks. You'll see..."

Chapter ELEVEN

Saturday dawned. Henrig and the children ate an early breakfast. Aunt Beastly had already headed off to work and without her it felt just like old times.

"I don't like our aunt," Scarlett announced. "She's hairy – and she smells of boar poop!"

"And Basil scares Coggs," Martha sighed.

"Please try to be nice to her," Henrig replied, passing round Bubblegum-flavour smoothies. "I know she can be a bit *determined*, but she's only trying to help."

"Huh!" Otto muttered under his breath.

After breakfast, they set off to the museum. It was closed to the public until ten o'clock, but Henrig was taking his children to see the elephant arrive.

As they hurried towards the staff entrance, three sets of eyes watched their every move...

Since yesterday morning, the Unstoppables had been parked near the museum, watching all the comings and goings with great interest.

Overnight their bright red campervan had been resprayed sky blue. This would throw any nosy parkers off their scent – particularly the Crumb boy, who Stinkerton had relabelled "the pesky pint-sized detective".

Stinkerton had already spied the walrus-woman march up earlier in what looked like a brand-new uniform. And now the rest of the family had rolled up, too.

As the Unstoppables watched, the side door of the museum opened and the Crumb family stepped inside, disappearing from view.

"A-ha!" said Stinkerton. "Lenny, Doug, I've

just had a brilliant idea! Why waste our time breaking into the Crumbs' house to get our hands on that hole when the walrus-woman will hand it to us on a plate?"

"Huh? I don't get you," Lenny shrugged, and Doug looked thick, as usual.

"Leave it to me!" snapped Stinkerton. "Just do what I say."

Inside the museum, Mr Doddery led the Crumbs along a narrow passage. "Let's see," he said, checking his watch. "It's three minutes past nine, so the elephant arrives in twenty-seven minutes' time! Why don't you have a quick look round while you're waiting?"

Henrig nodded. "Come on, children! I'll show you where the elephant will be on display."

He led the children to the entrance foyer and up a wide flight of stairs. Martha was looking out for fire exits (in case of dire emergency), Scarlett was wondering how slidey the banisters might be, and Otto was peering around for Aunt Beastly. He felt sure that she was up to no good.

On the landing beside a set of double doors was a sign saying "Indian Exhibition". Henrig held the door open and they went inside.

The room was filled with amazing Indian objects. There were delicate vases painted with elephants, ancient stone tiger statues and detailed models of temples and palaces.

But the children were more interested in their dad's case. It stood in the middle of the room, waiting for the elephant to arrive. Otto's fingers brushed the gleaming glass. Then Henrig proudly explained how it worked.

"See here – round the base – are little cannons," he said, "which are loaded with **Boom-Boom-Bloom Seeds**. At night, movement sensors will shine purple laser beams across the whole room. If a robber were to creep through the beams, those cannons would shoot out the Boom-Boom-Bloom Seeds – which would then be watered by sprinklers on the ceiling."

The children looked up to see rows of sprinklers above their heads.

"When the seeds are watered," continued Henrig, "they'll swell up instantly. In two seconds, they'll be the size of footballs, and a labyrinth of thorny vines will burst out of them – boom, boom, bloom!"

"Then what?" asked Otto.

"Well, then," said Henrig, "the robbers are trapped – they'll never get through the thorny

maze. And even if they did, they'd be faced with
my glass case. The glass is so strong that not even
a sledgehammer could break it!"

"Wow!" said the children. Their dad was so clever. He deserved better than a rotten double-crossing sister!

Just behind Dad's case, two large objects sat on the polished wood floor. They looked like small sheds but had silk drapes for walls and beautifully painted domed roofs.

"Those are *howdahs*," Henrig explained. "Howdahs are small Indian carriages that were placed on the backs of elephants. They carried wealthy people, or were used in hunting or warfare."

Between the howdahs stood two Indian mannequins, hand in hand. They wore fancy clothes made from wild silk and embroidered with golden stars and moons. At their feet was an information board explaining who they were...

> **Prince Chandra and Princess Heera**
> The golden elephant was a wedding gift
> from Prince Chandra to his beautiful bride.

For a while, the children wandered round the room looking at all the exhibits. If *only* they didn't have to worry about robbers this would have been a brilliant day out.

At twenty-eight minutes past nine, Mr Doddery appeared. The elephant was about to arrive!

As they hurried outside through the staff entrance, a smart black van was pulling up.

"This is it!" said Otto. "The elephant's here!"

Two security guards got out of the van, opened the back door and carefully took out a wooden box containing the precious elephant.

The guards carried it inside, followed by Mr Doddery and Henrig. Martha, Otto and Scarlett walked behind.

When they got to the Indian Room, Mr Doddery pulled on a pair of white gloves and opened the box. Carefully, he took out the golden elephant and placed it through the sliding window in Dad's case, on to the plinth.

As soon as his hand left the case, the window sealed itself – it was as if it had never been there.

The children watched, open-mouthed. This elephant was the most magnificent thing they had ever seen. It was made from pure twenty-four carat gold. On its back was a white-gold rug, covered in pretty moons made from clusters of diamonds.

"*Chandra*," said Henrig, "is the Indian word for *moon*."

As the children continued to gaze at it, the room filled with museum staff, including Aunt Beastly. Everyone "ooohhed" and "aaahhed" as they spotted the elephant.

"And are you *sure* the case is working?" Aunt Beastly suddenly piped up.

"Absolutely!" smiled Henrig. "It's one hundred per cent burglarproof."

Everybody clapped and Henrig beamed.

Otto glanced at his dad as he stood there proudly. This was his chance to show the world what a brilliant inventor he *still* was. Otto just hoped that nothing would go wrong.

While Henrig discussed a few things with Mr Doddery, Otto whipped his Solving Crimes Notebook out of his pocket and flicked to a clean page. "Right," he said to his sisters. "Keep a lookout for suspicious characters."

At ten o'clock, the crowds flocked into the Indian Exhibition. Aunt Beastly stood in position beside the case – she'd clearly impressed Mr Doddery with her knowledge about the elephant and its history and had been given a very important job.

Scarlett looked her up and down and

sniggered rather loudly. Aunt Beastly was crammed into a pale green uniform, at least three sizes too small. It made her look like an overripe gooseberry!

Scarlett laughed even louder though when a group of rowdy Brownies tore into the room.

"Stop! No! *Hands off the case!"* boomed Aunt Beastly.

More and more visitors piled in, and Otto tried to spot dodgy-looking people. The Unstoppables *had* to be here somewhere.

As the morning went on, Dad went off to do some paperwork with Mr Doddery, leaving the children to enjoy the exhibition. They kept a constant lookout for the Unstoppables but, so far, there had been no suspicious sightings.

As Otto scanned the room for the hundredth time, his jaw suddenly dropped. Aunt Beastly was deep in conversation with three strange men...

One of them was lanky. Another was short and fat. The third looked older – he had a thin pointy beard and wispy brown hair swept back in an arty ponytail.

All three wore black jeans and pink polo shirts with some sort of logo on the front. And the older man carried what looked like a large black camera bag.

"Look at those men," Otto said.

"What?" shrugged Scarlett. "They're just news guys. They're probably doing a story on the elephant."

"No," muttered Otto. "I don't think so. By the size and shape of them, I wouldn't mind betting that those three are the Unstoppables!"

"*The Unstoppables*," gasped Martha. "Do you really think so?"

"I'm sure," whispered Otto. "Just trust me. They match the descriptions of the other suspicious people we've spotted. We need to find out what they're saying. Come on!"

The children skirted round the crowd and slipped inside a howdah close to their aunt. The room was noisy and it was hard to hear exactly what she was saying. Her voice seemed oddly quiet – barely more than a whisper.

They caught the words, "*brother ... inventions ... cellar...*" before Scarlett suddenly blurted out, "Nasty double-crossing baddie!"

"Quiet!" hissed Otto. But it was too late. A podgy hand whisked back the curtain.

"*You!*" cried Aunt Beastly, her face flushing red. She looked fit to explode. "Out!"

The children trooped out glumly.

"You should know better!" barked their aunt. "Go and find somewhere else to play! Shoo!"

"What *now?*" wailed Martha as they headed on to the landing.

"We have to watch the robbers!" cried Scarlett.

"Yeah," said Otto. "But this time we mustn't be caught..."

For the rest of the morning they peeped round the door, tracking the robbers' every move.

At lunchtime, Aunt Beastly stayed on duty while the rest of the Unstoppables headed off to the café for some sandwiches.

Otto and his sisters were spying on them behind a big plant when suddenly their dad popped his head through the leaves.

"Whenever I lose you," Henrig grinned, "I always know Scarlett will be hiding out somewhere! So, what are you up to, then?"

"We were just playing!" Scarlett whispered quickly. The children's eyes flicked to the Unstoppables and back. Luckily Dad hadn't blown their cover, as the robbers still had their heads down, plotting.

Dad nodded. "Playing – I see!" he smiled. "Anyway, Mr Doddery has asked me to stay at the museum until it closes. Is that okay with you?"

"Absolutely!" said Otto.

"Jolly good!" smiled Henrig. "If you change your mind, your aunt finishes at one, so you could always go home with her."

He gave them some money for lunch and disappeared back upstairs. Shortly afterwards, the Unstoppables left, too. The children tailed them back to the Indian Room, where the gang disappeared into the crowds, unaware that they were being watched.

At one o'clock, Aunt Beastly's shift finished. As she headed out of the room, she was met by the Unstoppables. The robbers appeared to be going *with* her!

"Quick!" cried Otto, pulling his sisters with

him out on to the landing.

"Where are they going?" Martha whispered.

"To their secret hideout, I bet!" scowled Scarlett.

They watched them all head downstairs towards the front door. As they did, Otto picked back over the conversation he'd heard in the howdah earlier. "*Brother ... inventions ... cellar...*" he repeated. Then suddenly he gasped. "Wait! Dad's inventions! What if she's giving them to the robbers?"

"But why would she do that?" Scarlett frowned.

"I don't know!" Otto whispered. "Maybe she's hoping some of the inventions will help them steal that elephant."

"Beastly sneak!" Scarlett hissed.

"*We're doomed!*" Martha wailed.

"Come on," said Otto, "we need to get home before she gives them anything! Run!"

The children ran all the way back home. As they rounded the corner into Lighthouse Lane, they could hardly breathe. Then Otto saw a sky-blue campervan parked outside the house.

"Hey, what's going on?" he cried. "I'm sure that van was *red* yesterday – I recognize the flowery curtains! It was parked down our lane, then I spotted it in town. It must belong to the Unstoppables!"

"So that means..." said Scarlett.

Otto nodded. The Unstoppables were inside their house right now.

Chapter
TWELVE

Otto opened the gate and they hurried up the path. He edged open the front door as quietly as he could, and froze. There were voices coming from the kitchen.

"Otto, do you have a plan?" whispered Scarlett.

"I'm working on it."

"Maybe if we all did handstands?" said Martha.

"No!"

As the children stood rooted to the spot, Basil shot out of the kitchen.

"There, there!" cooed Aunt Beastly, bustling after him. "Those nice, kind men won't hurt Basie-Boo! Oh—"

She had noticed the children and stopped in her tracks. "I didn't expect you to be home so soon," she gasped, looking flustered.

"Well, we are," said Otto. "So, anyway, who have you got in the kitchen?" He shot his sisters a just-play-along look.

Their aunt sniffed. "Important guests," she said. "So just you mind your manners!" She turned on her heel and bustled into the kitchen.

The children followed her, Martha turning a wobbly cartwheel on the way. The kitchen table had been laid with the best china tea set and sitting round it, sipping tea, were the Unstoppables.

"This is Mr Smarmly and his colleagues!" beamed Aunt Beastly, as she fussed around them.

The children stared in disbelief. What were the robbers doing sipping afternoon tea? And what had happened to their aunt? She was giggling and twirling her hair round her fingers. And she was even *smiling*.

"More tea?" she simpered, her piggy eyes twinkling.

"No, thank you," said the man she called Mr Smarmly. "Though you do make a lovely cup of tea!"

"Mr Smarmly gave me a lift home," Aunt Beastly told the children. "He and his team are film makers! They also make documentaries about famous people." She glanced across to him and beamed.

"They're doing a film about Prince Chandra and his bride," she went on. "And guess what? They have agreed to do one about your *father*! The famous inventor, Henrig Crumb! I've been telling them all about him and they're very interested!"

"I *bet*," muttered Otto under his breath. Their aunt was clearly lying to them – yet again pretending to be "helping Dad out" when *really*

she'd brought her gang home to sneak them some of Dad's inventions.

Otto looked at the robbers – all three were shuffling about in their seats and glancing at the door. It was as if they were desperate to leave.

Hmmm, thought Otto. *Whatever they came for, they must already have.*

The one with the ponytail suddenly got up and said, "My dear lady, we've taken up enough of your time. We really must be going."

"But you can't leave yet!" giggled Aunt Beastly. "There's so much more to know, and I'm sure Henrig's delightful children could tell you so much more than I can."

"No way," roared Scarlett, "we're not telling that Un—"

"UNfortunately," Otto cut in, "we don't know a thing! Dad doesn't share his secrets with us."

The man's eyes flicked from Otto to the door and back to Aunt Beastly. "*Bessie,*" he purred. "Such a *pretty* name! It reminds me of a dainty rose."

Aunt Beastly blushed pink. "Why, thank you!" she replied, with a giggle.

"Why is she talking all ... *bleurgh*?" muttered Scarlett. "It's like she wants him to be her *boyfriend.*"

Scarlett gave a shudder. Boyfriends were totally *beastly*.

"You've given us all we need on your brother," the robber said nicely but firmly, "and now we must leave to write up our notes."

"So ... you don't need more?" Aunt Beastly sighed.

"No," he replied. "We've definitely got more than enough!"

Otto eyed Aunt Beastly. She must have given them some of Dad's inventions before he and his sisters had got home. And yet there were none poking out of the pretend camera bag. It wasn't even bulging. So where could his aunt and the robbers have put the inventions? Otto and his sisters followed them into the hallway.

"Goodbye, then," Aunt Beastly murmured.

"Farewell, dear lady," the man smarmed, kissing her hand. He opened the door and the robbers hurried out. "We'll be in touch! Thank you, *dear Bessie!*"

As soon as they'd gone, Aunt Beastly looked crestfallen. She scooped Basil up and headed off to her room, saying that she wouldn't be cooking dinner and didn't want to be disturbed.

"Oh dear, she looks really upset," said Martha. "I think she might have liked that man."

"Never mind *that*," said Otto, racing into the kitchen. "Follow me!"

He pulled open the cellar door, switched on the light and hurried down the steps, his sisters following behind.

"The Unstoppables must have swiped *something*, I'm sure! Why else would they be here? We need to check no inventions have been taken!"

They checked the cellar, then the rest of the house, but Dad's inventions all seemed to be there. It appeared the Unstoppables *had* cleared off with nothing.

As the sky-blue campervan sped away, Stinkerton opened his bag and carefully took out Rudolf.

"Huh!" he laughed. "Honestly, that was a total pushover! The walrus-woman fell for our story hook, line and sinker!"

"Yeah!" sniggered Lenny. "I *loved* the bit when you asked her if her brother had ever invented anything – say ... *invisible*?"

"Then she plonked that hole right in your lap!" snorted Doug.

Stinkerton stroked Rudolf's shiny blue frame. "Yes," he said in a silky voice. "Well, I've always been a genius. Did you hear how 'sweet' I was to her? Did you see how fast I whisked the hole into my bag the minute her back was turned?"

His eyes twinkled as he placed Rudolf down on the table beside his other robbing gadgets. If only he'd had this hole years ago. "Now stealing that elephant is going to be as easy as pie!"

That night, the children ate supper with their dad. Then Henrig went up to see his sister as the children did the washing-up. Otto washed, Martha dried and, as usual, Scarlett was doing the putting away. She opened the table drawer to get Rudolf but he wasn't in his usual place.

"Hey," said Scarlett, rummaging around. "Where's Rudolf?"

"I expect Aunt Beastly's tidied him away," sighed Otto. "I bet she thinks kitchen drawers aren't the place for magic holes!"

The children rummaged around in the drawer but there was no Rudolf.

Then, as they searched the kitchen, Martha suddenly yelped... "They've taken Rudolf to help steal that elephant! They'll use him to get through Dad's unbreakable case ... a-and the forest of thorny vines, too!"

"But," cried Otto, "how would they know what Rudolf can actually *do*?"

And then it came to all three of them.

"*Aunt Beastly must have told them!*"

Otto paced the floor. He'd been right! The Unstoppables had got exactly what they'd come for! Aunt Beastly must have given them Rudolf as soon as they'd got to the house. He'd been in their bag for the *entire* tea party! Now it all made sense.

"Right," said Otto. "If the Unstoppables have Rudolf, they'll try and steal the elephant *tonight*. We've got to stop them – we must go to the museum."

"But how will we get *in*?" Martha whimpered, whisking some fluff from her pocket.

"Dad's got some keys!" grinned Scarlett.

"I know where he keeps them!"

"But what are we going to *do*?" wailed Martha. "There's no way we can stop them on our own!"

"We can take some inventions to help us out!" said Otto, grabbing a rucksack off the back of a chair. "And I'll think up a plan."

They crept down to the cellar to see what inventions there were. Scarlett quickly found several pairs of **Day-for-Night Specs**. These looked like goggles but the lenses were made from special night-vision plastic, which allowed the wearer to see clearly in the dark.

"We'll take these!" cried Scarlett.

"Um," said Martha, "I think I m-might have something useful, t-too."

She held up a klaxon – a kind of loudspeaker with lots of buttons along the length of its handle.

Otto remembered it at once. It was called **Roary** and it made hundreds of different sounds. "Yeah, that might come in very handy!" he said. "Bung it in the rucksack!"

They also found a box of empty test tubes.

"Hey, we could use these to make stink bombs," said Otto. "Confusion tactics!" he added. "Now what smells really, really stinky?"

"*Aunt Beastly's perfume!*" Scarlett grinned.

There were also some bottles down there labelled **Bubbletastic Foam**, which were used in Wilma, the window-cleaning robotic elephant.

"I think we should take Wilma!" said Otto, a plan now forming in his head. "We'll confuse the robbers with the stink bombs and klaxon and they'll try to make a quick getaway. Then we'll floor them with a Wilma sneeze and tie them up with some rope!"

They had only just climbed back up the cellar steps when Aunt Beastly appeared in the kitchen.

"Have there been any phone calls for me?" she asked, her face still as glum as a raincloud.

"Nope!" said Scarlett, with a freckly grin. "Not one!"

Otto and Scarlett exchanged glances and Otto quickly mouthed the word "perfume".

He kept his aunt talking while Scarlett snuck off to the bedroom to pinch her stinky perfume. It was clear as they talked that his aunt was still very grumpy.

"So, are you feeling better?" he asked finally.

"Sadly, no."

Aunt Beastly plodded back upstairs as Scarlett returned with a bottle of the perfume hidden under her top. It was now nine o'clock and the sky outside was beginning to turn orange.

184

Dad came down to get a cup of tea and said that he was going to have an early night.

As soon as he'd gone back upstairs, the children brewed the pongy stink bomb potion. Then they quickly gathered up their things.

"But what if something goes wrong?" muttered Martha.

"Stop worrying," Scarlett tutted.

"Right," said Otto. "Time to go."

"No – wait!" cried Martha, grabbing a piece of paper. She wrote Dad a note explaining where they were going and what they planned to do. Then she tiptoed upstairs and popped it on his pillow as he snored.

"Come on!" said Otto, as Martha returned and Scarlett handed him Dad's museum keys. It was time to stop those Unstoppables once and for all...

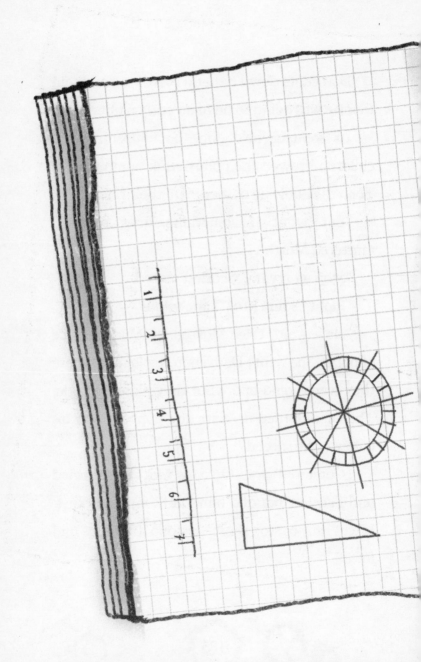

Chapter
THIRTEEN

As they headed off down Lighthouse Lane, Martha felt sick with worry. Even a fluffle-*whale* probably couldn't save her family now!

Scarlett, on the other hand, wasn't scared at all. Otto had said she could use Wilma to bring the robbers down, as she was the best shot by far, so she couldn't *wait* to get going.

As they hurried along, Otto slapped Ear, the tracker bug, on to Scarlett's back.

"Hey!" scowled Scarlett. "I don't need tracking."

"Oh, yes, you do!" said Otto, plugging Wig into the screen. "I want to know where you are when we split up in the museum."

They turned into Seagull Street.

"Listen up," said Otto, feeling just like his hero, Plum. "I've got a plan..."

Step 1: Otto and Martha hide in a howdah and wait for the Unstoppables.

Step 2: The Unstoppables arrive and, with the help of Rudolf, steal the golden elephant.

Step 3: Now that they have proof the Unstoppables are robbers, Otto and Martha deploy "confusion tactics" - Roary the klaxon will impersonate a police car as the perfume stink bombs come crashing down.

Step 4: The Unstoppables flee down the stairs (probably blubbing like babies!) where Scarlett is waiting to zap them with Wilma. They are quickly floored by gigantic sneezes of super-slippery foam!

Step 5: While the robbers are on the floor, Martha, Otto and Scarlett tie them up.

Step 6: Otto calls the police. The police arrest the robbers and they're carted off to jail. The Crumbs live happily ever after! Ta daa!

"That's not a bad plan," Scarlett said.

"I just hope it works," sniffed Martha.

"Don't worry," Otto nodded. "It will."

When they got to town, they hurried down Broad Street and round to the back door of the museum. Otto unlocked the door with Dad's keys and they slipped inside.

It was pitch-black inside the museum as the shutters were down. Otto found the Day-for-Night Specs and handed them out. Then they scurried along the maze of narrow passageways.

When they reached the entrance hall, Scarlett hid behind the ticket desk with Wilma.

"Stay put," said Otto. "You know what to do?"

"Sure do!" grinned Scarlett excitedly.

Otto and Martha hurried upstairs, but as they reached the Indian Room they stopped dead. The movement sensors were sending purple light beams across the entire room. They had forgotten all about these.

"What are we going to do?" whispered Martha. "If we touch *any* of these beams we'll activate the Boom-Boom-Bloom Seeds."

"We'll have to slither across the floor!" gasped Otto. He got on his tummy and pulled himself forward under the beams. Martha did the same.

When they reached the howdah they quickly slipped inside.

"Now we wait," said Otto. "Are you okay?"

"Um," Martha swallowed hard. "I, er – I think so. I just hope we don't get caught, that's all."

They waited. The stillness rang in their ears. They shivered, hardly daring to move. This had to work. It *had* to. For Dad.

It felt like they were squatting there for hours ... then suddenly they heard something.

"*Voices!*" breathed Martha.

"Yeah," gasped Otto. He shot a finger to his lips. "Shhh..."

"What a genius hole!" they heard a voice say. "Breaking in through that wall just now was a doddle!"

They listened as the robbers climbed the stairs, their footsteps getting louder.

"Martha, throw out the stink bombs when I say," whispered Otto. "Then I'll set the klaxon off."

Martha nodded, her eyes wide with fear and her face ghostly white. "Okay," she breathed. Her hands were trembling as she clutched the stink bombs tightly.

Otto searched down the klaxon's handle for the right button. He needed the scream of a police car. That would surely send any robbers into a spin!

The Unstoppables' footsteps stopped at the door and their torchlights cut through the darkness. Otto peeped round the drapes, watching them through the Day-for-Night Specs.

"Movement sensors!" the lead robber laughed. "Can't they do better than that?"

"Yeah," snorted the dumpy one. "Those daft beams of light never do a thing."

"Just there to try and scare us off!" laughed the lanky one.

"Yes, well," hissed the leader, "they don't scare *me*! Stealing this elephant is going to be easier than I thought!"

Laughing, the Unstoppables stepped into the room, but as they broke the purple light beams the cannons round the base of the case blasted –

BOOM, BOOM!

A shower of tiny seeds shot into the air.

"Now they'll be sorry..." whispered Otto. He saw the leader suddenly leap back.

"Blast! What's going on?"

Then the sprinklers began to rain down. As the water met the seeds, they grew bigger and bigger – until **POP!** The seeds burst and a tangle of thorny vines sprang out, twirling and writhing around Henrig's case and across the whole room.

"*Blimey!*" muttered the dumpy robber.

"Eeek!" gasped the tall one. "Run!"

"No!" hissed the leader. "I've got just the thing!" He shook out Rudolf's frame almost lazily. "How very entertaining!" he said, licking his finger and twiddling his bottlebrush moustache. Staying cool under pressure had made him what he was – simply brilliant!

He eyed up a nearby thorn and hooked Rudolf's frame over it. Immediately, a hole appeared through the vines and with it a long Rudolf-sized tunnel leading right to the case!

"*Whoa*," whispered Otto.

"What is it?" breathed Martha.

She peeped round the howdah's drapes to see the hole Rudolf had made in the vines. The fat one squeezed through first, then the other two climbed in after him.

As they edged their way along the tunnel the leader dragged Rudolf behind him. He needed Rudolf to get into the case, too.

When they got there, the leader popped Rudolf on to the case and a hole appeared through the glass. "How easy," the children heard him say. "We're there, boys!"

He plunged his arm straight through the hole

and his fingers closed round the elephant. How good it felt, so cool and expensive!

Then suddenly the fat robber shrieked. "Yikes! Them thorn things are growing again! How do we stop them, gov?"

The vines behind them had reappeared the moment Rudolf had been moved away and popped on to the case. Huge thorns were edging closer and closer by the second!

"Get the blasted hole on them!" the leader bellowed.

But first they needed to get the elephant out. Otto watched the leader whisk it from the case and stuff it into the loot sack. Now Otto had all the proof he needed to send the robbers to jail. He nudged his sister. "Now, Martha!"

"W-what?" Martha gulped.

"Chuck the stink bombs!" Otto whispered.

Quickly he and Martha tossed out the stink bombs. Five test tubes filled with pongy yellow liquid crash-landed on the floor with a splintering smash! The smell of Aunt Beastly's perfume immediately filled the air.

"Bleurggh!" gasped the dumpy robber.

"Yeuch!" heaved the tall one.

"*What the d-devil is going on?*" the leader spluttered. He grabbed Rudolf and slapped him back on to the tangle of thorny vines.

Then Otto let the klaxon rip.

WHOOO-OOO! WHOOO-OOO!

The sound was deafening!

"*Run for it!*" the boss robber yelled. "Listen!

The cops are coming. *Quick!*"

He dived through Rudolf and out through the door. The skinny robber raced after him.

"Hey!" puffed the dumpy one, bumbling behind and pulling Rudolf's frame with him. He quickly tossed it to the leader. "Hey, gov! *Wait for me!*"

There was hardly even time to blink before the robbers were speeding down the stairs. Otto grabbed Prince Chandra's jewel-handled sword and started chopping a path through the vines. Now it was all down to Scarlett...

As the robbers reached the bottom of the stairs, Scarlett gripped Wilma's trunk and leaped from behind the ticket desk.

"Take this!" she cried, her unruly red curls as wild as the look in her eyes. "And serves you jolly well right, you horrible baddies!"

Scarlett took aim and squeezed the trigger at the end of Wilma's trunk. A slurping gurgle could be heard as it filled up with soapy water, then...

WHOOSH!

A jet of foamy water blasted out, like a great, sticky sneeze. **WHAM!** It hit the lanky robber right in the face.

"Ho!" he shouted, tottering back as Scarlett quickly took aim again, and...

BAM! It smacked the fat one right in his enormous tummy.

The soapy water bounced in every direction, showering the place with super-thick foam.

"Stop that kid!" the leader yelled, as Wilma's suds jet-cleaned everything in sight.

A lake of frothy foam now covered the floor, making it as slippery as an ice rink!

"Help!" shrieked the Unstoppables, sliding around everywhere.

Otto and Martha appeared at the top of the stairs. They peered through the storm of bubbles and Martha gave a gasp. The robbers were finding their feet again. They were going to escape. The leader had managed to reach the front door. Martha watched as he slapped Rudolf on to it and a hole appeared.

He was about to scramble out when an enormous thing came flying through the hole.

"No, you don't!" the something boomed,

rugby-tackling the leader and bringing him down with a thud. The loot bag flew from his fingers and landed a little way off.

At that moment, *another* body flew through Rudolf yelling, "STOP! Don't you dare hurt my children, you ... criminals!"

"Dad?" called Scarlett through the bubbly fog.

"Where are the robbers now?" cried Henrig. "Goodness – I can't see a thing!"

"I'm here, too, Dad!" Otto shouted. "Me and Martha – we're coming to help!"

"Geronimo!" bellowed Martha bravely.

Batting away the foam, they headed downstairs.

"Scarlett!" cried Otto. "Turn Wilma down!"

"I can't!" yelled Scarlett. "Her trigger's jammed!"

"Lenny! Doug!" one of the robbers shouted.

"Somebody's got me! Ooof – they're squashing me flat! *Help me, you idiots! Quickly!*"

Dumpy Doug grabbed Lenny's arm and they scrambled through the bubbles. They threw themselves on to the foamy figure who was pinning their leader to the ground.

"Arrggh!" cried the mysterious figure.

"Who is it?" Otto cried. He tried to wipe the foam off his Day-for-Night Specs but it was hopeless.

"Otto!" Henrig called. "Where's the elephant?"

"Ow!" squealed Martha. She'd tripped over something and had landed on the floor. "It's here!" she shouted. "The loot sack's here!"

Martha went to grab it but as she did, Lenny and Doug fought off the foamy figure that was pinning their leader down.

He slithered free and quickly snatched up the loot sack. "Ha!" he cried triumphantly. "NOW, Lenny! Directions to the door!"

"What?" muttered Lenny, leaping to his feet and peering through the bubbles. "Three steps to the right then eleven steps forward ... I-I think."

The leader scrabbled to the door. Lenny and

Doug scrambled after him, but Scarlett wasn't giving up. Karate-kicking her way through the foam, she leaped on to the leader's back.

"You ... *baddie*!" Scarlett shouted, pinching his ears.

"Get off me!" he roared. "You vile little crab! Get off!"

"I think Scarlett's in trouble!" cried Henrig, blowing a big cloud of bubbles off his nose.

"Yeah!" said Otto. "Come on, Martha, let's find her!"

He grabbed his sister by the arm and pulled her along beside him. "NOOOO!" he cried, as they slipped in a pool of sticky foam and went flying.

As Otto stumbled to his feet he heard muffled voices near the door, then suddenly it went deathly quiet.

Out of the silence came the sound of a van speeding off down the road.

"*Scarlett?*" called Henrig. "Are you okay?"

But just then Martha gave a horrified squeak as a soapy figure staggered towards her. "S-Scarlett?" she muttered uncertainly. "Otto – i-is that Scarlett?"

But it was not Scarlett. It was...

"*Aunt Beastly!*"

Chapter FOURTEEN

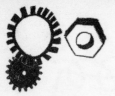

A unt Beastly had something in her hand. "The elephant!" Otto cried. "You ... you've *got* it?"

Aunt Beastly nodded. "That robber thought he'd got the better of me. But I snatched the loot sack during our scrap on the floor and managed to grab the elephant!"

"But ... but..." said Otto, almost lost for words. "Aren't you one of—"

Before he could finish, Dad appeared through the bubbles. He'd just managed to unjam Wilma's trunk trigger so she'd finally stopped shooting bubbles.

"Phew!" gasped Henrig, as the storm cleared.

Aunt Beastly shone her torch around. "Hold on," she said. "Where's Scarlett?"

Everybody looked around but Scarlett was nowhere to be seen.

"*Those nasty robbers!*" Aunt Beastly cried. "They must have taken her! Quick! We've got to get her back!"

Otto unlocked the front door with Dad's keys and they hurried out into the street.

"Into the car! Now!" boomed Henrig, sounding a lot like his sister. "And *when* we get Scarlett back, I shall want a full explanation of *exactly* what's been going on!"

They piled into the car, the golden elephant safely in Aunt Beastly's bag. Dad started the engine and tore off down the road. But when he reached the junction at the end he came to a halt. "How do we know where to go?"

"Wait!" cried Otto. "Scarlett's wearing Ear!" He pulled Wig out of his pocket.

"Look! I can see her on the screen – they're heading down Seymour Lane!"

"After them!" roared Aunt Beastly.

"After Seymour Lane, head down Rum Street," said Otto, "then left into Kipperjack Lane! That's where they are right now."

"Right," said Henrig, making a sharp right turn.

"*And put your foot down, man!*" cried Aunt Beastly.

As they weaved through the streets of Sharkstooth Bay, Otto noticed that his dad was still in his pyjamas. And so was Aunt Beastly!

For a moment Otto wondered if their aunt was just *pretending* to be good, as a cover story, but as he went through everything in his head, it was clear that she really *had* been trying to help them all along.

He'd been wrong, yet again. She had saved the elephant. *And* Dad's reputation. Their aunt had never been a robber at all.

"H-how did you know where we were?" asked Martha.

"I found your note," Henrig replied, "when Basil started howling for the loo. Just as well he did, or I might not have woken at all."

The note, Otto saw, was in the footwell of the car. He picked it up and read it...

Dear Dad,

We've had to go to the museum to stop the most notorious gang in the history of the world. Don't worry, we'll be all right (well, probably) although many, many things might go wrong. If they do go wrong and we never come back (for various different reasons) we want you to know that you've been the best dad ever.

love, Martha, Otto and Scarlett xxx

P.S. Please look after Coggs and make sure he never drinks from the kitchen taps, on account of the plughole goblins. Thank you.

Otto looked through the window. The sky was black. He hoped that Scarlett was okay. "Those robbers," he said. "They're not *normal* robbers."

"They're the *Unstoppables*," Martha whispered. "And, Aunt Bessie, we ... we thought you were one, too."

"Oh!" said their aunt. "Well, I'm not."

"Sorry!" cried Martha. "But you were telling them all about Dad's inventions."

"Because I thought those robbers were *film people*," Aunt Beastly explained. "I thought they could help your father, that's all. But now I know that I should never have let them into the house."

Henrig seemed very deep in thought as they rattled towards Kipperjack Lane.

"So the Unstoppables broke through my case then?" His voice sounded hopeless.

"Only with *Rudolf*, Dad!" cried Otto. "Only with one of *your* inventions! You're brilliant! And they could only do it because of you!"

Henrig was quiet for a moment. "Where next?" he said, sounding much more determined.

Otto checked the tracker. "They've stopped on a track near the cliffs, by the old castle. Head off to Puddleton Road, then out along Seathistle Street."

"Right you are!" Henrig cried.

"We will get Scarlett back, won't we?" sniffed Martha.

"Of course, we will!" Henrig nodded. "We're the Crumbs! *All* of us!"

"And Crumbs," said Otto, "will *always* stick together!"

Ten minutes later, Otto directed Henrig off the road and up a winding track. It was dark and the way was barred with cones. They crept from the car, moved the cones to the side, then drove along the track at a snail's pace.

At the end of the track they glimpsed the ruined castle. It looked dark and deserted. Henrig turned the car's headlights off so that the robbers wouldn't see them coming, and Otto and Martha popped their Day-for-Night Specs back on. Parked near the castle, they could see the robbers' campervan.

As they crept out into the night, Otto felt his heart thumping hard.

"I'll look around the front," whispered Aunt Beastly, "while you all check the back."

"No – I'll go with you," Martha said. "It wouldn't be nice to go alone."

"Oh," said Aunt Beastly with a little smile. "Thank you, Martha."

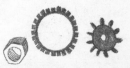

"There's nowhere to hide round here," whispered Otto, as he and Henrig checked the back. Where could they all be?

Then suddenly out of the corner of his eye, Otto spotted something. A tatty old barn, a little way off, up a grassy mound. And striding away from the door of the barn was...

"*Scarlett!*"

They hurried towards her.

"Look!" beamed Scarlett. "One of my wobbly teeth has finally come out!"

"Oh, Scarlett!" cried Henrig, hugging her. "Thank goodness you're all right!"

"Course I am!" said Scarlett, grinning. "I can look after myself! It's *them* you ought to be worried about!" She jerked her head to the old stone barn behind her.

"What?" whispered Otto. "The Unstoppables ... they're in *there?*"

"Yep!" giggled Scarlett. "But they're not going *anywhere*, don't worry!"

Scarlett then told them the whole story of how she, Scarlett Crumb, aged six and three-quarters had stopped the Unstoppables, *single-handed...*

"I was hanging off the robber man's ears when they raced out of the museum," she explained. "I wouldn't let go, so they bundled me into their getaway van. I think they were going to lock me in that barn, but I managed to lock *them* in instead."

"How?" gasped Aunt Beastly.

"Easy-peasy!" said Scarlett. "I was still wearing my Day-for-Night Specs, so while they were bumbling about in the dark in the barn, I let go of the robber man's ears and grabbed the loot sack, which he'd dropped on the ground. I reached in and... Well, the elephant wasn't in there—"

"No, *we've* got it!" Martha cried. "Aunt Bessie got it back when we were in the museum. *She* was the bubble-monster that rugby-tackled that robber."

"Really?" Scarlett grinned. "*Wow!* Anyway, where *was* I? Oh yes! The elephant wasn't in the loot sack, so I tossed the sack to the ground. Then, when the robbers made a dive for it, I karate-chopped my way to the door. *Yaah! Haa! Hoo!* So now I'm outside! Then I slammed the door shut and barred it with a branch. And now the baddies are locked inside! Ta-daaa!"

With that, they heard the sound of raised voices coming from inside the barn, followed by some curious groans. They clambered up the bank to investigate...

"Oooh! Ouch! Lenny, watch it! You're ripping my *robbing* trousers!"

"Well, you shouldn't be so *fat* then, should you?"

"Be quiet, both of you! One, two, three and HEAVE!"

Suddenly all went quiet. Otto pressed his ear to the door, but all he could hear was the rumble of the sea, until Martha's horrified shriek rang out...

"Look – down there! They're getting away!"

She pointed a trembling finger down the track as two headlights lit up the night. The Unstoppables were back in their campervan.

The engine roared into life and, a moment later, the sky-blue monstrosity tore off down the track.

"How did they get *out*?" Henrig gasped.

They unbarred the door and peered inside. On the far wall was a Rudolf-sized hole, and from it dangled a pair of large black trousers.

"Oh no! They still had *Rudolf*!" cried Scarlett. Yet again they had used him to escape. She sprinted into the barn and whisked him off the wall.

"Come on!" Aunt Beastly roared. "*After them!*"

"There's no way we'll catch up now, Bessie," said Henrig. "We've got no way of tracking them."

"At least we've got the *elephant*," Otto said.

"Exactly," Henrig nodded. "And right now we need to get it back to the museum and clear up the mess. Mr Doddery must never find out what happened, or I'll be out of a job before you can say *Crumbs*! Let's go!"

Everyone got back into the car and they rattled off down the track.

"We're going to be okay, a-aren't we?" asked Martha.

"Of course, we are!" Otto grinned. "We've saved the elephant, Dad's case is unharmed and the Unstoppables wouldn't dare come back now."

"Otto's right," said Henrig, "and most importantly, you're all safe. But you three have a lot of explaining to do. In the morning, I want to know everything that's been going on – from the very beginning. And I mean *everything*."

Scarlett gave a secretive smile. There was something she *wouldn't* be telling. For, during that scuffle in the barn, she *had* found something in the loot sack. Not the elephant, but a scrapbook. And nobody knew she had it.

When no one was looking, Scarlett edged out the book from under her top and read the words on the cover...

Sebastian Stinkerton
My Glorious Life in Crime

A tingle of excitement shot up Scarlett's spine as she slipped the book away. She had no idea what was inside but she couldn't *wait* to find out! It would be her little secret....

Follow the Crumbs
on their next adventure:

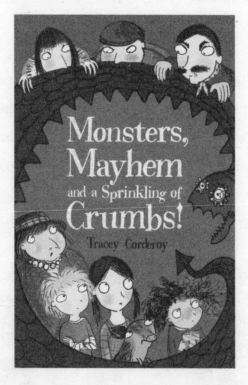

Coming soon!